A Granite Springs Christmas

A GRANITE SPRINGS NOVELLA

Maggie Christensen

To my wonderful husband and soulmate
who proved to me that it's never too late to fall in love.

Also by Maggie Christensen

Oregon Coast Series
The Sand Dollar
The Dreamcatcher
Madeline House

Sunshine Coast books
A Brahminy Sunrise
Champagne for Breakfast

Sydney Collection
Band of Gold
Broken Threads
Isobel's Promise
A Model Wife

Scottish Collection
The Good Sister
Isobel's Promise
A Single Woman

Granite Springs
The Life She Deserves
The Life She Chooses
The Life She Wants
The Life She Finds
The Life She Imagines

Check out the last page of this book to see how to join my mailing list and get a free download of one of my books.

Prologue

Magda couldn't believe her eyes. Her house, the home she'd lived in for more years than she cared to remember, was a smouldering mass. Her hand went to her mouth, her eyes filled with tears. She pushed open the door of her ute and jumped out, almost falling onto the hard-packed surface.

The lane was blocked with fire trucks, and she could see the yellow and red vests of the firefighters moving among the ruins. There was nothing left of the home she loved, the home that held all her possessions, all her memories. When she heard the news item reporting one house had perished in the blaze, she'd known it was hers. She'd left town immediately in the hope that…what – that she could save it? There was nothing to save. She could only watch the smoke rise and the few remaining flames being dowsed.

As she started to run towards the wreck of what had been her house, she stumbled and stopped, her hands going up to cover her face. She heard a loud wail, before realising it came from her. Magda gradually became aware of two men approaching her. One was her neighbour, Col Ford, and the other the man who'd recently moved into the house on a neighbouring property.

Col rushed over to hug her but, after a few moments, she pulled away. 'I'll be all right, now,' she sniffed. 'I knew… It's just… seeing this… But I'm okay. The dogs are okay. We were all in town. I just need to see to the horses.' She moved over to the fence, made a clicking sound with her tongue, and the three racehorses she'd saved from the knackers yard came galloping towards her from the far side of the paddock, only slowing when they reached the fence line. 'I'll be all right now,' she repeated, her eyes falling on the charred fenceposts which still held the sagging strands of wire. 'It's only stuff. It can be replaced.'

'Come with us, Magda, you can't stay here.'

She hesitated for a moment, then shook her head as another car drew up and an elderly man got out. Recognising her old friend, Magda turned to him with a sigh of relief. 'George,' she said.

'Come here.' He stretched out his arms.

But Magda was more intent on the horses.

'I'll see her and the beasts right,' George said to the two men. 'You guys need to check your own places.'

'Come on. There's nothing we can do here,' Col said to the other man, getting back into their car.

George took Magda in his arms. She began to shake, the full import of what had happened finally hitting home. Tears came to her eyes again and she brushed them away. But when the car had driven off, she finally gave way, slumping against her old friend, tears now streaming unchecked down her cheeks.

'There, there.' George patted her back ineffectively. But the touch of another human being brought a fresh bout of tears to Magda. She, who spent her life comforting others, who was quick to offer advice, even to predict their future, was at a loss when she was the one in need of reassurance.

'It's as if I've lost Bill again,' she sobbed, accepting the handkerchief George offered and wiping her eyes. 'He'd have hated to see all his good work disappear like this.'

'You're a strong woman, Magda. You'll get over this. Bill… he'd have fallen apart.'

'You think?' Magda rubbed her swollen eyes. 'You were always a good friend to him, George. And you have been to me, too.' She thought back over the years since her husband died, how George had always been there for her, for the boys. She knew what people said, the rumours that flew around about her and George, none of them true. He was a good friend, nothing more, even if sometimes…

'What'll you do now?' George's deep brown eyes met hers. They were filled with concern.

'I'll rebuild, of course,' she said without hesitation. 'This is my home. It'll be a good chance to put something modern on the old block, something that'll last me out. There's always an opportunity to build something out of the ashes of a disaster.' She managed a faint chuckle. 'And the amazing thing is that many of my plants look as if they've survived the blaze. It's uncanny, as if there was an unseen hand guiding it and protecting them. I'll still have my garden.'

'Right now, I mean. You can come back to my place…' George ran a hand through his still thick white hair. 'But I don't know…'

This time, Magda did chuckle. She knew the circumspect retired country town solicitor would be a target for the Granite Springs gossip mill if she spent even one night under his roof. Never mind neither of them would see seventy again.

'Thanks, but there's no need. I left the dogs with Mary. She's not so able to get around these days so didn't make it to the show. That's where I was when we heard the news of the fire.'

'Me too. I was worried you were here. I couldn't get out of town till now. I…' His forehead creased. 'I'm so glad you're okay, Magda. I don't know what I'd do if anything happened to you.'

A flash of something Magda barely recognised shot through her at the depth of emotion in her old friend's voice. 'I can stay with her for a bit,' she said huskily. 'And I suppose I'll have to call Kenny and Scott.' She sighed. Neither of her two sons had chosen to remain in Granite Springs. Her eldest had emigrated to Canada over twenty years ago and was settled there. Kenny, the younger one, though he was forty-four next birthday – how time flew – had taken off to the bright lights of Sydney as soon as he left school. Now he lived in Adelaide with his wife and three sons. He'd been agitating for her to move down there for some time now. No doubt he'd see this as a perfect excuse to further his case.

'How are the two rascals? I haven't seen them around here for some time.'

'No.' Magda heaved a sigh. 'Granite Springs wasn't big enough for either of them. Maybe if Bill had lived… I don't know…' She shook her head. 'But they're grown men now, George, with families of their own. It's up to me to visit them if I want to see my grandchildren.' And she did that so rarely Kenny's boys barely knew her, and Scott's two daughters were now practically grown up. 'I suppose that's what happens in families these days. It's not like it used to be.'

'You're right there. We stayed here, where we grew up. You must have been… what? Seven? Eight?'

'Eight.' Magda remembered it so well. How, as the shy little Magda Szabo, she'd escaped from Hungary with her parents to arrive in Granite Springs. To the young Magda, Granite Springs had been so alien. It had taken her years to adjust, but adjust she had and, grateful to the country and town that provided her family with a new life, safe from the aftermath of the Hungarian Uprising, from the nightmare of death and destruction, she'd never had the desire to live anywhere else.

'As I said, I'll be fine. It's a shock, but I'll get over it. I've survived worse.' The memory of the destruction they'd left behind in Hungary came forcibly to mind again. 'Mother and Father had more than this to deal with. They lost their home, their family, many of their friends and their country. I've only lost a house.' The tears began to flow again at the thought of the memories her house contained. It was all very well to dismiss it as *stuff*, but it was the stuff of memories. But, she reminded herself, the most important memories were the ones she held in her heart. No one could take them away from her.

One

Magda gazed out the kitchen window across the paddock to where three horses grazed on the short grass. She stroked the surface of the newly finished kitchen bench with her veined hands before turning, her eyes moving across the kitchen, through the open plan living and dining area, to the front yard where the plants that survived the bushfire were still flowering. Some would have said it was a miracle the lavender, mint and thyme were still alive, and Magda would agree. She firmly believed there was a higher power watching over her; the same power that had saved her and her parents all those years ago, and brought them to this safe haven; the same power that gave her the strength to face each new day with the conviction that all would be well.

It had been good of Kenny and Laura to take her in when the old place burned down almost exactly a year ago. Despite her initial reluctance, she'd finally agreed she needed to get away, needed time to regain her equilibrium after the shock of seeing her home of so many years devoured by flames. And it had been good to spend time with the family. But after several months with Kenny and his family, during which she managed to sort out insurance issues and remotely arrange to have a new home built, she'd needed a break from her overly protective son and his kindly but patronising wife.

The email from Canada had been a godsend. She'd enjoyed her few months with her Canadian family, developing a special bond with her nineteen-year-old granddaughter, Holly, who reminded Magda of herself at the same age.

But she was glad to be back in her own home – her new home. Her children had their own lives and, much as she loved them, she'd missed Granite Springs and her independence.

Once the formalities had been taken care of, it hadn't taken long for the demountable to be erected on the site of the home she and Bill built when they were newly married, when this ten acre block seemed like heaven and a good place to rear their family. It had been all of that, until Bill was killed in a freak accident at the abattoir when Scott and Kenny were still in primary school. But then, as now, she'd soldiered on, setting up a massage business in a spare bedroom to help make ends meet and to enable her to be there for the children when they came home from school.

Magda, after making sure the dogs had food and water, wandered through to her new custom-built massage studio. This was one of the many advantages of her new home and the one of which she was most proud. Over the years, she'd built up a large number of clients for her massage business, many of whom she now regarded as friends. And if she sometimes offered her clients the odd prediction of the future couched in terms of well-intentioned advice, what harm was there? Her mother always told her she had a bit of the gypsy in her and she knew her family were descendants of the Roma. But that was several generations ago. When younger, Magda's thick dark hair had been a legacy of this, but now while still thick, her crowning glory was pure white – or silver as she sometimes called it with a touch of unaccustomed vanity.

It would be Christmas in two months, and she wanted to spend it in her new home. This year she'd be the one to provide Christmas with all the trimmings. She thought back to that horrible experience the previous year when she was living with Kenny and Laura. They'd invited Laura's family to Christmas lunch, and Magda found herself stuck in a corner with Laura's aged mother who suffered from dementia, and practically ignored. For the first time in her life, Magda felt old. It was something she never wanted to experience again. She was only seventy-one, and had lost her home, not her faculties.

Thinking of Christmas and celebrations reminded Magda of the message her neighbour had left on her phone last night. Jo Ford had been one of her first massage clients and, living just along the lane, they'd become friends, Magda's son, Kenny and Jo's Danny being around the same age. The two boys had been forever getting into mischief together when they were in primary school.

Magda made a pot of peppermint tea and spread some toast with the ginger marmalade Laura had insisted she bring back from Adelaide. Despite Magda's insistence she could buy it in Granite Springs, Laura had pressed the homemade confection on her, along with several other grocery items. Kenny's car had been bursting at the seams, but it had been good of him to bring her and the dogs home again, and of Mary to let her stay until her new furniture was delivered.

She took her breakfast out onto the veranda, breathed in the air filled with the scent of gums she'd missed for the past year and picked up her phone.

'Magda! How lovely to hear from you. Thanks for returning my call. I thought it best to let you have a few days to settle in before calling. Remember we talked about having a celebration once you got back?'

Magda racked her brains. She recalled having tea with Jo and Fran, another client, before she left town. Had there been mention of a celebration? Perhaps. She'd had other things on her mind that day, not least of which was Fran's future, which she'd seen so clearly as they sat together over cups of herbal tea. It was something she couldn't explain, this ability to see things that were about to happen. Sometimes she wished she didn't have it, but she knew it was a gift, one she had to use wisely.

But it never worked for her own life. Maybe that was for the best.

'I do remember some mention,' she lied. 'But a celebration sounds a bit over the top.'

There was a pause before Jo spoke again. 'Nothing big. But perhaps…' Jo paused, as if working out how to respond. 'I did tell you Owen bought the Kelly property and he and Fran are living there now?'

Magda smiled. She'd known that would happen long before she heard it from Jo. 'You did. I was so pleased. They belong together.' She nodded to herself and took a sip of tea.

'Yes, well… Anyway, I thought I'd invite them. Would that be all right? And would you like me to invite George Turnbull? I know you two are friends.'

George. Dear George. Magda knew she should call him. But something was holding her back, a hesitation she was at a loss to understand. When that sort of thing happened to her – and it didn't happen very often – she always found it best to wait. The universe had a way of sorting things out for her.

Now she said, 'That would be a good idea, Jo. Thanks for thinking of him.'

'Is there anyone else?' Jo asked.

Magda thought for a moment before replying. There were so many people in Granite Springs for her to contact again, but she had no intention of allowing Jo to invite them all. 'Perhaps my friend, Mary,' she said at last. 'She's been kind enough to put me up both after the fire and when I came back again. She's on her own and I'm sure she'd appreciate the invitation.'

Magda realised she was on her own too, though she never thought of herself that way. She was always busy, never lonely. How could she be lonely with Caesar and Brutus for company and her three horses to take care of?

After arranging for the get-together to be held that Saturday, Magda finished the call and sat for several minutes contemplating how lucky she was and how rich her life. Recognising her mood, Caesar and Brutus came over to push their noses into her lap.

'Oh, you dears.' She stroked their silky heads. 'You're glad to be home, too. Now, I do have one more thing to do before we go for our walk.' It was time. She picked up her phone again and hit speed dial.

'Hello, George, I'm back!'

Two

Magda was back!

When he received her email, giving the date of her return to Granite Springs, George felt his heart skip a beat. He might be in his seventies, but he had the heart and mind of a much younger man and his body was in pretty good shape, too, even his hair was still as thick as when he was younger.

He was sure Magda never guessed how he felt about her. He'd been Bill's friend – good old George, always there to lend a hand and to comfort her when things got tough. And it had started out that way, but somewhere over the years his feelings had morphed into something more. But he'd managed to hide it under a gruff manner, only giving way to his emotions when he was alone.

Initially, when the boys moved away, he wondered if perhaps things might change between them. But Magda was busy with her massages and the other nonsense women got up to, and he'd had his legal practice and his position as director of the Granite Springs Choristers which he set up when he was in his thirties. Now retired from both, time hung heavy on his hands.

What he needed was a hobby. He'd never had need of one till now, always busy with one thing or another. There was his garden, of course, but even that didn't require much of his time. He'd never taken to golf like many of his legal colleagues. He'd even found himself wandering into his old office, much to the irritation of young Bruce Jenkins, whose practice it now was, forcing the man to take him out to lunch in an attempt to get rid of him. Recently, he'd joined a family history group at the library in the hope the search for his family tree would fill some time. And he'd bought himself a few orchids and set them up in a greenhouse in the backyard, hoping learning about them would fill some of the empty hours.

He was fixing himself a coffee and preparing to spend the day searching on the Ancestry website to put into practice what he'd learned, when his phone rang.

Hearing Magda's voice again was music to his ears. He'd missed her over the past year, their only contact a few texts and emails. Plus, of course, the photos she posted on Facebook of her family and the beautiful scenery around Adelaide and Victoria on Vancouver Island where she was spending time with her sons. At various times, he'd wondered if she might decide to change her plan to rebuild here in Granite Springs and stay with one of them. But it hadn't happened. She was back home and calling him.

'Magda, welcome back. Everything good?'

'Everything's very good. It's so lovely to be back. I missed my home, George. Family are all very well, but they have their own lives and there's no room in them for me.'

'I'm sure that's not true.' George couldn't imagine Magda's two boys shutting their mother out of their lives. He'd known Scott and Kenny since they were born, sometimes felt he was as much their dad as Bill was. They took the place of the children he'd never had himself.

'Well, maybe not precisely. Both of them suggested I move to be closer to them. But what would I do in a retirement village in either Adelaide or Victoria? They're both lovely places but it would drive me mad in a week.'

George chuckled, both with relief at her return and the thought of Magda in a retirement village. 'You'd brighten them up for sure.'

'Anyway, I'm back now. Caesar and Brutus are as happy to be home as I am.'

'Why don't we go out to dinner – to celebrate?' George held his breath waiting for Magda's reply. Going out to dinner wasn't one of their things. Coffee perhaps, from time to time, but mostly they met at his home or hers. Halcyon always reminded him of Bill and the times the three of them spent there together. Bill always thought it a stupid name for the property, but Magda had insisted, saying it signified peace and joy and was the name of a mythical bird. As in everything else, she got her way. That was the thing about Magda, it was hard to resist her. She never appeared to be aggressive, but her calm manner concealed a steely determination.

'I'd love to see you, but dinner? That sounds very flash. I just spoke to Jo Ford. She wants to organise some sort of celebration for my return, too. On Saturday. You're to be invited.'

George thought quickly. He knew the Fords. They were good people. Col had been a solicitor colleague before both of them retired. It would be nice to see them again and a good idea to celebrate Magda's return. But he didn't want their reunion to be in the company of a group of other people.

'Sounds good. But why don't we go to The Riverside on Friday? You can tell me all the family news then. I know we emailed, and I've enjoyed all the photos you posted online, but I'm sure there's a lot you didn't say – that you can't tell anyone else.'

Magda gave a throaty chuckle. 'You know me so well, George. And we go back so far. I'd love to give you the lowdown on my two reprobates and their families. But be prepared. I love them all dearly, but they're no saints.'

'They never were.'

'You're so right. Oh, it's so good to talk with you again. I can't wait to let my hair down and fill you in on what I've had to put up with. So, Friday?'

'At the Riverside,' he repeated. 'I'll make a reservation and meet you there at seven. It'll be good to see you again.'

'Me, too.'

George hung up. His coffee had gone cold, and the Ancestry website no longer seemed attractive. All he could think of was the diminutive woman with wild white hair who'd agreed to have dinner with him on Friday evening.

Three

Magda had spent the afternoon with the horses, the dogs lolloping along behind her but managing to keep out of the way of any stray hooves. They'd learned that lesson early. The former racehorses didn't mean to do any harm, but they sometimes forgot they were retired and out to grass, and liked to kick up their legs as if they were still young and sprightly. A bit like me, Magda sometimes thought. She could probably do a few high kicks herself if she was so inclined.

She took one last look around the house before she left. Her two greyhounds were lying in their favourite spots, one on either side of the Aga. It had taken them no time to feel at home again, and it never ceased to amaze Magda how they always chose the same spots, never trying to oust each other.

Wearing one of the few dresses she possessed – a simple royal blue shirtdress with three-quarter sleeves – and having made sure the dogs had plenty of food and water, she was ready to leave. As she put the ute into gear, she reflected how right Kenny had been to insist she replace the battered old Holden she'd driven for years with this new model Toyota Hilux with a bright blue cab, though she had to admit the choice of colour was hers. Blue was a colour that was calm and relaxing; it projected peace and confidence, and was one of her favourite colours. Of course, she hadn't told Kenny all that. It would have reinforced his belief she was away with the fairies and should definitely be shut up in some retirement village to moulder away her twilight years. Instead, she just said she liked the colour which, rolling his eyes at the salesman, he'd accepted as being one of her quirks.

This was the first time Magda had driven it into town and she was once again surprised and pleased with the smoothness of the transmission. Maybe Kenny had been right, though she'd been sorry to lose her old friend. It had served her for more years than she cared to remember. She recalled how she and her two boys often squeezed together on the bench seat when they were little and how, in more recent years, Caesar and Brutus joined her, much preferring the comfort of the cab to rattling around in the tray.

She was still reminiscing when she pulled up beside The Riverside and, hopping out, spied George stepping out of his white Prius. She smiled to herself. He was so proud of that car – what he called his way of doing his bit for the environment, as if one car would make a difference. But that was one of the things she admired about him. He had a conscience.

Catching sight of her, George hurried over to give her a hug and a peck on the cheek. It was how they always greeted each other, always had, even when Bill was alive. No wonder there were rumours about them, rumours that amused them both.

'Welcome back,' he said.

'Missed me?' Magda asked, jokingly. 'You didn't find yourself a woman while I was away?'

George blushed.

She really shouldn't tease him like this.

'Of course I've missed your sharp tongue,' he said without missing a beat. 'You know how I like grumpy old women.'

'Less of the old.' They both laughed and walked into the restaurant arm-in-arm. That would give the gossips something to talk about.

Once they were seated with glasses of the house red – neither made any pretence of being a wine aficionado – they made their choice from the menu. Magda chose the vegetable risotto while George settled for lamb shanks served with couscous and broccolini.

'This is so nice.' Magda sipped her wine and gazed around the room, recognising several of her clients enjoying a Friday evening out. She must contact them, let them know she's back in business. But not till next week. Tonight was for enjoyment, not business.

Looking across the table at the craggy face of her old friend, Magda knew she'd made the right decision to come back to Granite Springs. Though really, she'd never considered any other option.

'Penny for them?'

'Oh, just pleased to be back home, and with you, dear friend.' She raised her glass. 'To old friends.'

'Old friends,' George repeated, raising his in return.

Did Magda detect a cloud in his eyes?

'So, what were my godsons up to?' he asked, when they'd been served and taken their first taste of the delicious meals.

Magda laid down her cutlery, smiling across at him. When Bill suggested his old friend as godfather for both their sons, she'd initially wondered if it was a wise move. But, over the years, especially since Bill's death, he'd proved to be, if not a substitute father, a wise counsellor to both of them, until his advice was no longer heeded.

'Much the usual. They're dear boys, but as they've grown, they've both become unbelievably pompous, believing they know what's best for me. If Kenny had his way, I'd be locked up in a retirement village on the outskirts of Adelaide with he and Laura visiting when it suited them.'

'And Scott?'

'Not quite so bad.' Magda grew thoughtful, picturing her older son as he'd farewelled her at the airport. 'His heart's in the right place, and Tara's a much gentler person than Kenny's Laura. She'd be easier to get along with – and Holly and Chloe are delightful, but… it's so far away and it wouldn't be my own home.' She gave George an apologetic look. 'I've grown set in my ways. I like to be with my dogs and my horses – and I enjoy my own company. I can't wait for you to see what I've done with my new place. Thanks so much for taking care of all the arrangements for me.'

'I didn't do much. Young Bruce took care of all the legal stuff. I did wander out a few times to make sure the construction was going according to plan,' he admitted. 'You chose a good design. It fits in with the area and your neighbours. You're happy with it?'

'Very happy. I think Bill would have liked it, too.' Magda was silent for a moment, remembering the love of her life who'd been cut down in his prime. As manager at the abattoir, he had no need to be down on the floor, to be near the machinery that caused his death. They'd never know what prompted him to be there on that day, at that time. She gave a sigh, and George reached his hand to cover hers.

'He was a good man, sorely missed.'

'Yes.' She gave herself a shake and picked up her cutlery again. 'What I want to do, George, is have a really special Christmas this year. I plan to invite both boys and their families to spend it at Halcyon. You'll come too, won't you? It'll be a big family celebration, like we used to have when they were younger.'

'Sounds like a great idea.' George took a gulp of wine. 'It won't be difficult for them all to get away or too much work for you?'

'Of course not! I'm their mother. And, after last Christmas I spent with Kenny and Laura, anything would be a breeze. I can always get this place to provide the food, if I do get stuck.'

'No doubt about you. But was last Christmas so bad?'

'You don't want to know.' And Magda had no intention of regaling him with the appalling details. 'Sufficient to say I won't be repeating it – ever. I can visualise it clearly. I want it to be like it was when the boys were growing up – ham, turkey with all the trimmings, a big tree, decorations, the whole catastrophe. It's only two months away. I can't wait.'

'Sounds wonderful. If there's anything I can do to help, you have only to say.'

'Thanks. There will be. I know it's a huge undertaking on my own. With the two of us, it'll be six adults and five children, though Scott's two don't think they're children any longer.' She grinned remembering her Canadian grandchildren who considered themselves quite grown up.

'And they'll all come?'

'Of course they will!' But Magda's confidence wobbled for a moment. She'd broached the idea with both her sons while staying with them and they'd told her they couldn't wait to see her new house. Kenny had already had an advance viewing when he brought her back home, but that was before the furniture arrived. It had been an empty shell – and he'd been itching to get back on the road. But all of the grandchildren had been delighted at the idea of a Christmas at Nana Magda's new house, even if Laura had made noises about her being too elderly to take on such an undertaking.

'Kenny's Laura did make some remark about elderly women,' she said, chortling. 'I do hate that word, don't you?'

George smiled in agreement. 'I heard a few people mutter it when I resigned from my position as director of the Granite Springs Choristers.'

'Who's taken over? Not that dreadful Ron Harris, I hope,' Magda said, referring to the bumptious music lecturer at Willian Farrer University who'd had his eye on George's position for years.

'Luckily not. Young Owen Larsen has proved to be a blessing to our community. He didn't need to be persuaded to take over. He's shaken them up a bit, while keeping to the traditional offerings for our Easter and Christmas performances. He'll be a good neighbour to you, too – him and Fran.'

'She's such a lovely lady. I was so pleased they got together. I don't know much about his background, but Fran has been a client of mine since she arrived in Granite Springs. I'd like to think she's a friend too. They'll be at this do of Jo's tomorrow.'

'He's a damned good musician, a composer, too. And he's as happy on that property as a pig in muck.'

'You don't regret giving up the choir?'

George seemed to consider the question before replying, 'Sometimes. But I knew I couldn't stay with it forever. It was time to move on, make way for a younger man. I was just glad Owen arrived in town when he did. Otherwise…' He shook his head.

'So, a family Christmas,' he said, harking back to their earlier conversation. 'It'll be good to see the young ones again.'

'You never regretted it? Not having children?' It was something Magda had often wondered but never asked. She wasn't sure why she was asking now. It was as if some unseen force was putting the words into her mouth.

'No.' George gave a sigh. 'I guess it wasn't to be. I told you about Rose – the girl I was in love with at uni. When that didn't pan out – when she went back home to New Zealand to care for her mother – I never felt the same about anyone else. Anyway…' he grinned, '…your two almost made up for it. It was good of you and Bill to share them with me.'

'It was good of you – especially after Bill… There was many a day when I don't know what I'd have done without your help. I always appreciated it, George.' Magda's voice was tender.

She looked at her companion. He was such an important part of her life. He and Bill had been best mates since they were at primary school together. It was a friendship that had withstood the test of time, of George going off to uni, of Bill being sent to Vietnam when he was scarcely old enough to hold a rifle. George had been a support for her then too, she remembered. Then, when Bill died, it was George who'd been there to pick up the pieces, to deal with the legal issues she was too distressed to handle. And he continued to be an important part of her life – of their life. He'd been more than an honorary godfather to her two sons, Their Uncle George was the one they turned to when they were bullied at school, when their teams made the finals, when…

She was lucky to have such a good friend.

Four

Back home, George poured himself a glass of whisky and settled down in front of the television. He was too wound up to go to bed. But, after flicking through the channels, he decided there was nothing worth watching and turned the set off again to gaze into space.

He'd been surprised by Magda asking him about children. It was something he'd often thought about. There was something sad about being alone at his age, but it was of his own choosing. He'd spoken the truth when he said Rose had been his first love, but lied when he said there had been no one else. Maybe that was the moment he should have come clean, but the words stuck in his throat. What if Magda laughed at him? What if it spoiled their friendship? No, better to leave things as they were.

And it wasn't as if he'd become a hermit after Rose left him. There had been others, both at university and when he returned to Granite Springs. As a young solicitor, then the director of the Granite Springs Choristers, there had been many women who'd been happy to spend time with him – and more. And he'd shamelessly taken advantage of some of them. But those days were gone, and he had no regrets. Well, as the song went, only a few to mention, one of them being the lady he'd spent the evening with.

He was glad Magda seemed to have recovered from the shock of losing her home. She was an amazing woman. And to be planning a big Christmas celebration… He hoped she was right about her family being willing to come to Granite Springs. God knows, they hadn't been the best at keeping in touch over the years. Many were the times Magda had confided in him she hadn't heard from either of them for weeks or even months. 'I could be lying there dead for weeks and they'd never know,' she said once, in a fit of frustration. Then she'd have a long Facetime conversation with one or other of them and all was forgiven. Maybe that's how it was with families.

George finished his whisky and was debating whether to pour another or go to bed. He knew that, on top of the wine he'd drunk with dinner, another dram would most likely mean he'd have a restless night, when his phone rang.

'I trust I'm not calling too late for you,' Owen Larsen said, the hint of a chuckle in his voice. 'I don't want to be a bother.'

'You could never be that, Owen.' George leant back in his armchair, wishing he had poured that second glass. A call with Owen was never brief or boring. Since he'd arrived in Granite Springs to take up the position of Head of the School of Music and Drama, Owen had made both the university and everyone he met uneasy with his laidback attitude, his casual appearance, and his innovative ideas. So much so that the students called the new school The Mad House – a name he was proud of, but which was frowned on by the powers that be in that academic establishment.

'Let me get a refill, then we can talk.' George set the phone down, went over to the sideboard to refill his glass, then returned and picked up the phone again. 'Now what can I do for you?'

'What are you drinking?'

'I have a glass of ten-year-old Glenfiddich.'

'A man after my own heart.' Owen chuckled. 'I wanted to talk with you about the choir's Christmas performance.'

'You are planning to do the Messiah again?' George felt his heart drop at the thought Owen might be about to change the age-old tradition. He knew the younger man had his own ideas about what was appropriate and wanted to put his own stamp on the group, but had hoped some things would stay the same.

'Of course. I wouldn't dare change that. But I did wonder if you'd be willing to sit down with me to work out the program and perhaps come along to the first few rehearsals. You know how easily I can get carried away. Fran's always telling me I should think before I speak or act.'

It was George's turn to chuckle. He could picture Owen with his untidy grey hair, his face screwed up in an anxious frown, sitting in his rocking chair by the Aga. He'd managed to tidy himself up somewhat after he arrived in town, but was fast returning to his earlier state of dishevelment. Even Fran didn't appear to be able to keep him in order. He had what George would call a true creative personality.

'It would give me the greatest pleasure. I'd be delighted.' The thought of being involved again in what had been one of the true joys of his life filled George with pleasure. His face broke into a smile. 'Christmas isn't too far away.' He remembered Magda's plans. 'When did you have in mind?'

'Oh…'

George realised Owen hadn't thought that far ahead.

'Can you come to rehearsal on Tuesday… and maybe get together with me sometime before that?'

'You haven't started rehearsing yet?'

'Well… a bit, but I need your input.'

George sighed. It was typical of Owen to start something, then ask advice. But he didn't mind. It was exactly what he needed – a project to keep his mind active and to stop him wondering about Magda. He thought quickly. 'There's this barbecue at the Fords tomorrow – to welcome back Magda Duncan – your neighbour. I'll be in your neighbourhood. I could drop in afterwards if that suits – or would you prefer me to come to the campus?'

'Perfect! I seem to recall Fran telling me about the barbecue. It's tomorrow? We'll be there, and you and I can have a chat afterwards.'

When the call finished, George sat for a moment, rolling the now empty glass in his hands. What a surprise. It was good Owen believed he still had something to offer, and it would be good to see the choir he still thought of as his again. It was around this time last year he'd decided to hand over to Owen. Last year's performance of The Messiah had been his last as choir director. He knew it was the right thing to do. He didn't regret it. But it had left a gap in his life he hadn't been able to fill.

Castigating himself for being a silly old man, then retracting the word *old*, he rose unsteadily and took his glass into the kitchen, glancing out the window to see a full moon shining down on him. It sent his thoughts back to Magda, making him wonder if she was gazing up at that same sky, making him hope she'd enjoyed the evening as much as he had. And he had tomorrow to look forward to – to seeing Magda again, to the meeting with Owen, to the prospect of being involved with the choir again, albeit in a small way. Perhaps life wasn't so bad after all.

Five

Magda opened her eyes and stretched, dislodging Caesar and Brutus who had taken advantage of her pleasure in being home to sneak into her bedroom and onto her bed. The morning sun was peeping through the white plantation shutters she'd chosen as window coverings and leaving strips of sunlight on the pale green carpet to give it a dappled appearance.

Her thoughts returned to the previous evening. It had been good to see George again, her George as she often called him to herself, though he was really Bill's George. She wondered what her life would have been like if her beloved husband had lived. Would she have started her massage business, or would he have dismissed the idea as one of her airy-fairy notions? He'd never been comfortable with what he called her mystical meanderings. He'd doubtless have slotted massage into the same box. She thrust the thought to the back of her mind and focussed on the day ahead.

After brewing a cup of peppermint tea and feeding the dogs, Magda showered and dressed before heading off with them across the paddock. Once she'd checked the horses, she called the dogs, who were sniffing around the fence line, and set off down the lane, the greyhounds at her heels.

This was Magda's favourite time of day, when the dew was still hanging on the grass like diamond droplets and the birds were in full song. As they made their way over the uneven ground, she gave thanks for whatever force had helped Bill and her find their block of land in the first place, and allowed her to rebuild her home after the fire.

She laughed as she always did, to see Owen's goats, some grazing peacefully, others leaping around, while still others were intent on pulling down low-hanging branches. Looking closely, she noticed several kids lying with their mothers. Owen had been busy while she was gone. He must have brought in a billy. She called back Caesar who had drifted close to the fence. It would never do if he got into the paddock with the goats and caused havoc.

Further along the lane, she passed Yarran, the property where the barbecue was to be held later in the day. Col Ford was already out there with his new herd of alpacas. When Magda left, he'd been undecided which type of animal to purchase. Jo had kept in touch and filled Magda in on his decision. The alpacas had been a good choice. She was lucky to have such good neighbours.

Back home again, Magda prepared breakfast. It was good to be able to return to her old habit of homemade muesli with fruit and yoghurt. The difficulty in being a guest in her sons' homes had been having to eat with the family and to share their food. Neither Tara nor Laura had understood her desire to make her own healthy meals. Instead, she'd been forced to politely eat the pre-packaged breakfast cereals and – in Laura's case – the frequent takeaway meals they were accustomed to.

Breakfast over, Magda went through to her new massage studio, where her new laptop sat ready for use on a new white desk in the corner. Everything new, a fresh start. It was time to get back to work. Fortunately, all her business documents had been saved on the cloud so survived the fire. One piece of Kenny's advice for which she was grateful.

The morning passed quickly, the dogs lying at her feet in a pool of sunlight. She'd normally banish them from this room but didn't have the heart this morning and found their company comforting.

Around eleven-thirty, dressed in a pair of smart jeans and a blue and white striped shirt, Magda threw a navy sweater over her shoulders. She tied the sleeves in front and, picking up a bottle of chardonnay from the newly filled wine rack, told the dogs to stay and set off down the lane.

Her friend Mary's little Kia passed her on the way, and the two women waved to each other, Mary waiting at Yarran's gate till Magda arrived and opened it for her. She pushed open the car door when the gate was closed again and invited Magda to hop in.

'I'm glad to see you,' she said. 'I don't really know these people. Are you sure this is all right?'

'Of course,' Magda reassured her. 'Jo Ford is one of the friendliest people I know. There'll only be a few people here. I told her I didn't want a big celebration.'

As they drew closer to the house, Magda saw a line of parked cars. This wasn't what she expected. Wait till she spoke to Jo! But she smiled to herself at the thought so many people wanted to welcome her back.

She stepped out of Mary's car to a bevy of cheers and shouts of 'Here she is!', making her want to dive for cover. While it was nice to be appreciated, Magda had never been one for big crowds, preferring her own company or that of a few close friends. Her eyes were blurring with tears of either joy or embarrassment – she wasn't sure which – when there was a familiar voice in her ear.

'Come along, Magda. They won't eat you.' George took her by the elbow and steered her forward to where the large group of friends, clients and acquaintances stood waiting to greet her.

To Magda's surprise, she enjoyed the afternoon. After the initial shock, it was lovely to see so many people she knew and to catch up with what had been happening in Granite Springs while she was away. As the afternoon progressed, the groups mingled and changed, Jo's old Labrador, Scout, making his way between groups and stopping to sniff at Magda's heels, no doubt wondering where her two greyhounds were.

'Oh, you lovely old thing,' she said, bending down to scratch his head in a spare moment, before she was drawn into another group who wanted to know when she would be resuming her massages.

It was a relief to finally sit down beside Fran and Jo with a glass of wine and a plate heaped with salad and a piece of barbecued chicken.

'Lovely to see you back,' Fran said, raising her glass to toast Magda. 'We missed you, not only because I had to find someone else to give me my regular massages. Believe me, there's no one quite like you. And you were right about changes in my life.' She glanced fondly across the yard to where Owen was talking with a group of the men, holding a bottle of beer, waving wildly as he made his point. 'He was my light at the end of the tunnel. Thank you.' She gave Magda a kiss on the cheek. 'I didn't believe you. I was so lost in my past. But you knew better. Now I have a husband and a family.' She pointed to where a young woman was feeding a young child.

'Owen's daughter?' Magda guessed. 'Does it make up for...' She peered at Fran who lost her own child.

'Not entirely, but I do love them both.'

Glad to see Fran so content, Magda thought of her own family, wishing they lived closer. But she knew they'd never move back, and it was her decision to return to the town that had offered her and her parents refuge.

'How are your family?' Fran asked, as if reading her mind.

'They're well… and I'm planning a big family Christmas.'

'Oh, that sounds wonderful,' Fran said.

It did sound wonderful when spoken aloud. And while mindful of what she recognised as George's doubts, Magda firmly believed that if she spoke and thought about it often enough her ambitious plan would be achieved. If she closed her eyes just a little, the crowd in Jo's yard disappeared to be replaced by Scott and Kenny, along with their families. She was standing in her own backyard surrounded by her own family, Caesar and Brutus sniffing at their heels and the horses standing by the fence hoping for some attention.

Six

'Shall we walk up to my place or do you prefer to drive?'

Most of the guests had gone, leaving only Owen, Fran, George and Magda, when Owen took George aside. Glancing at Magda who was chatting happily with Jo, George answered that he'd say his goodbyes and drive up.

'See you shortly, then.' Owen waved towards Jo and Magda then, with a few words to Col, he and Fran set off towards the lane. His daughter had disappeared earlier with her little one.

'You're not going, too?' Jo came over to where George was standing undecided, and Magda followed.

'I should be getting back, too, Jo,' she said. 'There are the horses to feed… and the dogs…'

'I suppose so.' Jo sounded regretful. 'It's been a good afternoon. Thanks for coming, George.'

'Wouldn't have missed it,' George said honestly. While the gathering had been much larger than he anticipated, he'd known almost everyone there. 'Thanks, Jo. It was a suitable welcome home for this little lady.'

'Less of the little.' Magda drew herself up to her full height which must have been all of five foot four – he'd never been au fait with the metric system. She laughed, her eyes twinkling as she looked up at him. 'But I agree with George. Thanks for today, Jo. Though I'm not sure I forgive you for turning it into such a big do.

'Bye, George. Thanks for coming.' Magda gave him a peck on the cheek and set off towards the gate before he could offer her a lift.

Sometimes she was too damned independent. He'd have welcomed an opportunity to have a chat and rehash the event. But any such discussion would have to wait till another time.

At Owen's, he found Fran trying to maintain order out of the chaos created by Owen, his daughter, Pia, and one small child, while a black cat prowled around, mewing piteously.

'Hi, George,' she said, greeting him at the door. 'Owen, why don't you take George into your music room. I'll bring in coffee, and the two of you can talk in peace while Pia settles Tor, and I see to Stormy,' she said referring to the baby and the cat.

'Good plan. Through here, George.'

George followed him into a spacious room at the back of the house. The wall of bookshelves indicated it had been designed as a study, but it now contained a keyboard, a guitar, and several pieces of sheet music were scattered on a desk by the window. There were also two comfortable chairs. Owen took one and gestured to the other.

George took the indicated seat and gazed around the room. 'Nice place you have here.'

'I like it.' Owen stretched out his legs, crossing them at the ankles and George saw he was wearing an old pair of trainers. Owen didn't change. 'Now,' he said, 'to business.' He searched among the sheet music lying on the floor beside his chair, finally seeming to find what he was looking for. 'Here it is!'

The next hour was taken up with Owen outlining what he had in mind for the Christmas performance and seeking George's advice. Their conversation was only punctuated by Fran's arrival with two mugs of coffee.

What Owen suggested was innovative and would probably set tongues wagging, but George agreed with his ideas. 'It's time for a bit of a shake up,' he said. 'And you're the one to do it. I'm not sure what help I can be.'

'I need you to be there – at the rehearsals.' Owen pulled on a strand of his hair which George noticed was now almost long enough for him to tie back again in the man bun he wore when he first came to town. 'Fran is on at me to get a haircut,' he said, clearly seeing George's eyes on him. 'Maybe for Christmas.'

Everyone seemed to be preparing for Christmas, George thought

– first Magda, now Owen, even the shops were beginning to display Christmas food and decorations. It was a time for families, for celebration. It was a time when George always felt more alone than at any other time of year. In years gone by, he'd had the Messiah performance to look forward to, and he and Magda had fallen into the habit of having a meal together. But this year, with her family all here, it wouldn't be the same. Even if she invited him on Christmas Day, and although he knew her boys well, he'd still feel the odd one out.

But – he perked up – at least he was to be included in the preparation for the Messiah, even if it wasn't his choir any longer. 'I'd be glad to be of whatever help I can,' he said.

It was dark by the time George left Owen's, having refused Fran's offer of dinner. He was eager to get home to go over the score Owen had prepared and perhaps do some work on it before Tuesday's choir practice. But, as he drove into the lane, George glanced up towards Magda's property and, seeing her lights shining out into the darkness, felt drawn towards them.

Standing outside the door, George felt foolish. What was he doing here? He was about to turn around when he heard the dogs bark and knew it was too late. If he left now, Magda would know. Feeling even more foolish, he knocked on the door. Unlike the one on Magda's old house, this one was painted bright purple and had a flannel flower etched into a glass panel on the top half. Through it, he could see Magda approach.

As soon as she opened the door, letting the light from indoors spill out onto the veranda, the two dogs wound themselves round his ankles, greeting their old friend. They hadn't forgotten him.

'I thought it was you,' Magda said with a wide grin. 'I've just put a quiche in the oven. It'll be ready for us in half an hour.'

George shook his head. He'd never get used to this side of Magda – the way she seemed to know what was going to happen before it did, or was it only guesswork? She couldn't have known he'd drop by tonight. He hadn't known himself. And yet something had pulled him towards her friendly lights, something akin to the magic that emanated from her.

'Quiche sounds good. How did you know…?'

Magda only tapped the side of her nose with one finger and led him inside. 'First, let me take you on the grand tour,' she said as, the dogs following close behind, she took him through every room in the house finishing in the modern kitchen which held the familiar aroma of Magda's herbs with a hint of lavender.

'What do you think?' They were seated at the kitchen table with glasses of white wine. Magda had pulled the quiche out of the oven and served up two large helpings.

'The quiche smells delicious and the house is a masterpiece.'

Magda chuckled. 'It is, isn't it? The house, I mean. It's exactly the way I imagined it, even better than the old place, although…'

'I know.' George smiled tenderly. 'It's not Bill's.'

'No,' Magda sighed. 'But he's still with me, in here.' She put a hand to her heart and closed her eyes for a second. 'Now, we should eat.'

It was a surprise when, after the meal, as they were relaxing with cups of peppermint tea, Magda said, 'Tell me about your Rose.'

George almost leapt out of his seat. Where had that come from?

Seeing his shocked expression, Magda added. 'I feel her presence with us tonight. Don't you?'

'No. I don't share your… whatever it is.' George ran a finger around the inside of his collar. He didn't dispute these feelings of Magda's. The earlier reference to Bill had been bad enough, but when they related to him…

'You met at uni and…?' she continued, as if he hadn't spoken.

George could see she wasn't going to give up. 'We sat together in class and, one day, we got talking. It went on from there. We were close, very close.' George could still picture Rose with her long, straight, auburn hair, hair which swung on her shoulders as she bounced around campus in a skirt so short it was almost indecent. But that had been the fashion.

'You intended to marry?' Magda probed.

It was a long time ago. Why was Magda raking it up now?

George remembered how in love they'd been, how he wanted to get engaged, had even chosen the ring and been about to ask her when… 'I did, but I didn't get the chance to ask her.'

'What happened?'

'She had a call from home, from New Zealand. Her mother was ill, dying. She left straight away. We didn't even have time to say goodbye.

She left me a note.' George felt his stomach clench, much as it had that day, reading her brief note written on a sheet of lined paper hastily torn from a notepad. It was like reliving it all over again.

'She didn't come back?'

'No.' The bitter taste of Rose's rejection was still in George's mouth. It had taken him weeks to get a proper night's sleep. He'd almost failed his finals. But for the influence of a good friend, he might well have done so and ruined his whole future. 'I wrote to her, of course I did, but I only got one reply. She said things had happened there, things she couldn't talk about, and she had to stay.'

'What did you think?'

'She'd found someone else. That was the obvious conclusion. So, I locked the memories away and got on with my life, came back to Granite Springs, set up in practice, and here I am.' He looked across the table at Magda. 'You're a bit of a witch, Magda, to get me talking about Rose like this. I haven't ever told anyone what I just told you.'

She only grinned. 'People tell me things. And I tell them things, too. George,' she leant forward. 'I think there's news coming to you from New Zealand.

Seven

It was time to start baking for Christmas. Magda knew some people said six weeks prior was the optimal time to bake the Christmas cake, but Nigella recommended twelve weeks. She normally followed Nigella's recommendations, but since she'd just returned, ten weeks would have to do. It was close enough and she'd feed it with brandy in four and six weeks' time.

It was really beginning to feel like Christmas, and Magda began to hum her favourite Christmas melodies as she measured out the flour, dried fruit and sugar, opened the tins of chestnut puree and beat the eggs before simmering the dried fruit, butter, zest, rum and orange juice. Then she prepared her large cake tin, carefully covering the base with greaseproof paper and wrapping it around the sides. By the time the eggs, flour and spices were added, the kitchen was filled with the heady smell she remembered.

Once the cake was in the oven, Magda called to her dogs. In the two hours it would take to cook, she could take her usual walk around the lanes and be back in plenty of time. This was when she liked to think. Over the years she'd discovered the tranquillity of trekking along the lanes, past paddocks of grazing sheep and goats – and now Col's alpacas – was a time when she could let her thoughts wander.

Today, Christmas was on her mind and she determined to email both her sons when she got back. Then she planned to update her Facebook page. Over the past year, while posting scenery on her profile, she'd set aside *Massages with Magda*. It was time to resurrect her business.

A woman with a child in a stroller was coming out the gate at Fran and Owen's. 'Hi, Magda.'

'It's Pia, isn't it?' Magda stopped while the dogs sniffed the stroller, their noses investigating its occupant, to the delight of the little boy who chortled and waved his arms around.

'And this is Tor,' the young woman said. 'May we join you?'

It took Magda only a moment to agree. While she regretted losing the solitude of her walk, something told her the woman was seeking guidance.

They walked along in silence, the dogs ambling by their sides with the occasional foray into the rough grass along the fence line.

'Fran tells me you're a masseuse.'

'I am.'

'Would you… can I make an appointment? I feel I need… I don't know… I…'

Magda's insight told her Pia was in need of more than a massage. Had Fran also told her how Magda could help heal troubled souls? She could tell Pia was in dire need of help. 'I've not really started up again yet, so have plenty of time. Why don't you give me a call to arrange one? Bring this little one if you like. He'll be quite happy in a corner. You can be the first to experience my new massage studio.'

'Really?' Pia let her breath out. 'I'd like that. Dad told me you lost your house in the bushfire. That must have been dreadful.'

'We were all spared. I'm grateful for that. There's always something to be grateful for.'

'I suppose.' Pia's forehead creased.

'Is there something worrying you, Pia?' She saw Pia glance towards her son. 'Is it something to do with Tor?'

'Fran warned me about you,' she said, turning red. 'She told me you'd see right through me. It's about his dad.'

'He's not around?'

Pia shook her head. 'He threw me out when he learnt I was pregnant, but… now Tor's actually here, I wonder if it's fair to him – to Tor – to allow him to grow up without knowing his father. There's a young girl I met earlier who…' Pia bit her lip. 'She couldn't rest till she found out what happened to her dad.'

'How old is this girl and what were the circumstances?'

Pia thought for a moment. 'I think she's fifteen or sixteen and… her mother had just died.'

'A bit different to your situation, then,' Magda said gently, feeling compassion for the girl. Pia was probably in her late twenties but still a girl to her. 'It doesn't sound as if Tor's dad would welcome any involvement in his life. May be best to wait till he's older, see what he wants to do then?'

Pia gave a sigh of what could only be relief. 'Do you think so? That makes me feel so much better. I was worried that… You see, Darren lives in Sydney – that's where my life was before this one came along. But I don't think I could bear to go back there, not now.'

'So you'll stay here in Granite Springs, with your dad and Fran?'

'In Granite Springs, yes. But not with Dad and Fran. Oh, they've been so good to me, putting up with me and Tor and telling me I can stay for as long as I want. But I know I need to stand on my own two feet. I know of a place. I have a friend who's moving out of her townhouse. Sally helped me, gave me good advice when I was pregnant. Now she's in a relationship and is moving to live with him on his family property. She says I can take over her lease. It's a good opportunity…' Her voice trailed off.

'But you're not sure?' Magda guessed. 'It's a big step.'

'Yes!' Pia lifted her chin up determinedly.

'Have you thought of what you might do… to earn a living?'

Pia looked down at her hands clutching the handle of the stroller. 'Sally's been a big help there, too. She suggested I speak with her partner's dad. He's a local realtor. It's not quite what I was doing before – I was in recruitment – but she said he might have a vacancy. It would be a start.'

'I think that sounds like an excellent idea. Seems to me you have it all worked out. And Tor?'

'I still have to work that one out, but Sally says there are some good crèches in town and perhaps I can arrange flexible hours – you know, work from home some days.' Pia was looking brighter. It seemed talking about her situation had helped.

But something was worrying away at the back of Magda's mind, something to do with Pia's words about Tor's dad. It made her think of… no, it was gone again.

Eight

George was happily working on the score Owen had given him when his phone rang. Cursing silently at the interruption, he almost let it ring out, but the habit of a lifetime took over and he answered.

'Hello,' he said, distractedly.

'Mr Turnbull, George.'

'Bruce.' Why was his former employee, the man who'd taken over his practice several years earlier, calling him? He no longer had any ties with the business, and they'd been colleagues, never close friends. 'What's up?'

'George, sorry to bother you, but I received a strange call. The person wanted your contact details, but I thought I should check with you first. I didn't want to presume.'

Bruce Jenkins was a good solicitor, but had always tended to be over cautious, maybe not such a bad thing. 'Who is this person who wants to contact me?'

'That's just it. He didn't say. He was calling from New Zealand.'

George felt a chill run up his spine. The only person he knew in New Zealand was Rose. But that had been fifty years ago. This could have nothing to do with her, could it?

'He didn't give a name – state his business?'

'He refused. Said he'd only speak with you. He was quite insistent, almost rude.' Bruce paused. 'He said he'd call back. What shall I tell him?'

'I suppose you'd better give him this number,' George said slowly.

He was curious as to what this stranger might want with him. But, as he put down the phone, he remembered Magda's comment – about news from New Zealand – and a shiver ran through him.

He tried to refocus on what he'd been doing when Bruce's call interrupted him, but it was no use. He couldn't concentrate. He went to the kitchen and brewed some coffee. While the machine was gurgling and hissing away, he stared out the window to where a pair of king parrots were vying with each other for the seeds on the wattle trees at the edge of his backyard. They were beautiful birds, bright red and green plumage, the male with his red head, and the female with her green one. But today, even they failed to distract him.

What had happened to bring back memories of Rose – memories he'd thought banished forever into the recesses of his mind? It had been Magda, with her damned questions. But what had prompted her to ask him about Rose after all these years?

He could see Rose now, her dainty figure, her cheeky grin, hear her voice with that New Zealand twang he'd teased her about, feel her soft body against his, smell… This had to stop! It all happened fifty years ago. Even if she was still alive, Rose would be in her seventies by now. The young girl he remembered was long gone, and she'd been gone to him for all that time. You couldn't turn back the clock, and he wasn't sure he'd want to, even if he could. He was a different person from the naïve young man who'd made passionate love on the university campus, seized every opportunity to be with the girl he'd planned to spend the rest of his life with.

He was just settling down with his coffee when the phone rang again. Taking a deep breath, George picked it up.

'Mr Turnbull?' The voice, in the New Zealand accent, was modulated, educated and tentative.

Although he'd been expecting the call, and knew it was coming from New Zealand, it took George by surprise. He didn't answer immediately.

'I'm George Turnbull,' he said after a brief pause.

'I think you may be my father.'

Whatever George had expected, it wasn't this. He felt his world tilt sideways. His eyes blurred. He couldn't speak.

'Hello? Are you still there?' The voice seemed to come from far away.

George realised he was still holding the phone, gripping it so tightly it was pressing into his palm. 'Yes, I…'

'I realise this may come as a shock. It was a shock to me, too. My mother died recently and…'

'Your mother?' George had the strangest feeling. His chest tightened. Was he having a heart attack?

'My mother, Rose Howard. I'm Guy Howard.'

'I'm sorry, I…'

'Sorry, she was Rose Baker. I think you knew her at university in Sydney, back in the seventies.'

This was about Rose, his Rose. But what made this young man think he was his son?

George cleared his throat. 'I did know a Rose Baker at Sydney University, but what…?'

'Look, I'd rather not try to explain over the phone. I have to be in Canberra on business next week. Would it be possible to meet you? I can explain then.'

When George put down the phone five minutes later, he had more questions than answers. But he'd agreed to meet this man who claimed to be his son at his hotel in Canberra the following Monday. Guy Howard had promised to fill him in then. Though how he was going to make it through an entire week till then, George wasn't sure.

*

At least the prospect of the choir next evening gave George something to occupy him. He managed to spend the day working on the score for Owen, impressed by the innovative way the younger man put his ideas together. They were lucky the university had attracted him to Granite Springs, and that he was willing to put his considerable talents to use for the community.

After procrastinating all day, George finally picked up the phone to call Magda. He'd been stewing on the call from Guy Howard and wanted her take on it, even though he knew she couldn't be of any help. No one could.

'Hello, George.' As always, Magda's voice had a calming effect on him, making him wish he'd called earlier, perhaps even the day before, instead of delaying.

'Magda, remember you mentioned New Zealand?'

'Yes?'

Did he detect a hesitation in her voice?

'I received a strange call from this guy – called Guy, as a matter of fact.' He gave a wry grin. 'Says he thinks I'm his father.'

There was a pause, then, 'And what do you think?'

'I don't think anything. It's a crazy idea. How could I be, unless…?'

'Unless your Rose was pregnant when she left. I presume you and she…'

'Yes, we were sleeping together,' George said, irritated at having his earlier love life open to scrutiny, forgetting this was Magda who knew him inside out – well, not entirely, it seemed. 'But I'd have known.'

'Hmm.'

'Surely if she'd been pregnant, that would have been all the more reason to reply to my letters?'

'You'd certainly think so.' Magda seemed to be being particularly obtuse today. 'What are you going to do about it?'

'I'm meeting him. In Canberra. Next week.'

'Well, then.'

George didn't know what he expected from Magda – perhaps the opportunity to discuss the call. Certainly not what appeared to be a disinterested response.

'Go with an open mind.'

George waited, but she didn't say any more. 'Right,' he said. 'Have to go.' He hung up, disappointed both with Magda's response and his own reaction to it.

The choir practice was a joy. It was delightful to be back again with the choristers he'd led for so many years plus a few new members he didn't recognise. The new arrangements were enthusiastically received, and both Owen and George were complimented on the changes to the traditional program. 'All Owen's doing,' George admitted, deferring to his companion, who shook his head in denial.

It wasn't till he was home again, and the euphoria of the evening had left him, that George remembered Magda's closing remark. Open mind – what had she meant by that? And, for the first time it hit him.

What if this Guy person was right? What if he was his father? What if Rose had borne a son – his son? How would he feel about that?

Nine

Magda had barely got off the phone with George when it struck her. Now she knew what it was that had niggled her when she'd been chatting with Pia. It was the image she'd seen when she and George were talking almost a week ago. She'd seen him, so clearly, the young man who looked just like George, except for the hair. He'd had auburn hair.

It was unusual, even for Magda, to see what was in the future so clearly. Perhaps it was because she and George were such close friends, or perhaps it was just the way of things. She'd learnt never to question those things she sensed or, more rarely, saw. She'd also learnt to keep quiet about them, only referring to them in generalisations, or in well-meaning and carefully worded advice. And, for the most part, it worked. It had worked with Jo, and Fran, and numerous others. But, till now, she'd never seen anything for her old friend, George.

Perhaps that was why she'd been so hesitant to say much when he rang to tell her about his strange call. Now she knew what it was about, but only vaguely. She had no idea of the details of what she sensed, never did. If indeed the caller was George's son, his long-lost son, the son whose very existence he had been unaware of, how would he react? Would he be joyful or bitter? Was the man's mother still alive – the Rose that George had spoken of; the woman she'd felt it imperative to ask him about? Had that been preordained, too?

Consigning all thoughts of George to the back of her mind, Magda prepared her massage studio for her first client. It would be lovely to start with Pia. Since Magda had updated her Facebook page the day before, *Massage with Magda* had been inundated with messages from former clients seeking to set appointments, all eager to see the new studio. Magda had taken a photo with her iPhone and set it up on the page as a drawcard. It seemed to have worked. Now she was ready to get to work again.

*

When Pia arrived, she wasn't alone.

'We met on the lane and I offered to take Tor for a walk while Pia is with you,' Jo said, smiling. 'I miss the time when my lot were this size, and even the grands are getting bigger and are all at school now apart from Emily Rose. We love them and do everything for them, then they grow up and leave us. Enjoy him while you can,' she advised Pia. 'I'm right, Magda, aren't I?'

'You certainly are. But I think Pia has some time to enjoy this little one before he flies the coop. We'll be about an hour. And why don't you stay for a cuppa when you get back?'

'Will do. Enjoy your massage, Pia. I'll see you both in an hour. Come on, little man. Let's go visit the horses.' Jo wheeled a gurgling Tor off, her old Labrador, Scout, at their heels.

Caesar and Brutus whined at the sight of their friend leaving.

'You've had your walk,' Magda reminded them, then relenting added, 'But perhaps I can find you a biscuit. You'll have to stay in the kitchen while I'm with Pia. Come on through,' she said to Pia.

Entering the studio lit only by a dim table lamp and candles, Magda breathed in the familiar scent of lavender, geranium and bergamot. Soft music was playing from the playlist she'd carefully put together earlier.

Pia gazed around. 'I feel more relaxed already,' she said, smiling.

Magda chuckled. 'Just wait till we've finished, you will feel so much more than relaxed. I'll leave you to get settled.' She withdrew, closing the door behind her.

Back in the kitchen, she took a couple of dog biscuits from their container and gave them to the dogs, who settled happily in their spots by the Aga. Then she scrubbed her hands thoroughly before going back to join Pia.

The hour passed quickly as Magda firmly but gently massaged all the knots out of Pia's body. Then Pia sat up slowly, blinking as her eyes gradually became accustomed to the dim light.

'Take your time,' Magda said, handing her a glass of water. 'Come through to the kitchen when you're ready. Jo will be back soon, and we can all have tea.'

She headed through to the kitchen where she let the dogs out. Seeing Jo wheeling the stroller toward the house, Scout padding along beside her, Magda put the kettle on.

'Thanks so much, Magda. I feel wonderful.' Pia appeared, looking very relaxed, just as Jo arrived at the door with a fractious Tor. 'Oh, poor baby,' Pia said, picking him up and giving him a cuddle. 'He's teething. I won't stay for tea, Magda, if you don't mind. I'll get him home and see if he'll settle and have a nap. Maybe another time?'

'You've worked your magic again, Magda.' Jo left Scout outside with his friends and took a seat as Magda placed two cups of sweetly smelling camomile tea on the table along with a plate of brownies.

'She's a lovely girl. I'm so glad Fran and Owen have her and Tor with them, though maybe not for much longer.'

'I think not. She's young and will want to spread her wings. But I hope she'll stay in Granite Springs. It's a good place for children to grow up.'

'I think she will. It worked well for us, didn't it?' Magda joined Jo at the table and offered her the plate of brownies.

'Delicious,' Jo said, taking a bite. 'Been cooking?'

'Oh, they're not mine. I stopped into The Bean Sprout this morning and picked them up. I can't match Marie's brownies,' she said, referring to the woman who ran the popular café in Granite Springs. 'But I have made a start on my Christmas cake.'

'You're ahead of me. I can't think of Christmas till November at the earliest. I think we should be like America. I know several people there who don't begin their Christmas preparations until after Thanksgiving.'

'Mmm.'

'What are you doing for Christmas this year?'

'I'm planning a big family Christmas, like it used to be when the boys were little.'

'So, Scott and Kenny are coming home for the holiday? Danny will be pleased. He was disappointed he didn't see Kenny when he brought you back.'

'No. He was in a hurry to get home to Adelaide. Hopefully, Christmas will be different. We can do something together.'

'Sounds good.'

They sipped their tea, the silence only broken by the hum of the refrigerator, the snuffling noises from the dogs outside the door, and noisy squawks from the birds in the line of trees on the driveway. Surprisingly, many of the trees had survived the fire, and those which hadn't were already throwing out green shoots of new growth.

Magda twirled her cup around, wondering if she should confide in Jo. Usually the boot was on the other foot, and it was Jo asking for advice from her. 'I'm worried about George,' she said at last.

Jo raised an eyebrow and put down her cup. 'Is something wrong?'

'No. Yes. It's difficult. I… we…' She sighed. 'I know what people have been saying about us for years. It's not true. We're friends, good friends, that's all. Neither of us have ever wanted anything different. But since I got back, something's changed. I can't explain it. I just sense the difference.'

'You're the one with second sight,' Jo chuckled. 'Doesn't that tell you what's changed – as you put it?'

'No.' Magda sighed again. 'It's never worked for me, only other people. Probably just as well. And I did see a change for him. It's already happening.'

'So?'

'It's not to do with me.'

'Oh!'

Magda studied Jo's kindly face and made a decision. 'His long-lost son has turned up out of the blue – well, from New Zealand.'

Jo almost choked. 'Not another one!'

Magda flinched. How could she have forgotten the drama. It was a couple of years ago now that the illegitimate daughter of Jo's ex-husband arrived in town unannounced. That had set the cat among the pigeons. But all had been resolved, and Sally was the girl who had befriended Pia and who was now in a relationship of her own.

'Sorry, Jo. I didn't think. I didn't mean to bring up the past for you.'

'Oh, it was nothing to do with me. And Sally's turned out to be a blessing. But, this son of George's…?'

'He isn't sure the man is actually his son. He's gone to Canberra to meet him, to see if…'

'But you know that he is?'

Magda nodded. Sometimes she wished she didn't have this gift. She'd seen the auburn-haired man, the younger version of George, so clearly. 'It was when he was at uni. The girl went home to New Zealand. They lost touch. Poor George. He loved my boys as if they were his own. He'd have made such a great dad. He's always wanted…'

'Well, maybe now he can be. This son of his would be…?'

'All of fifty. A bit late in life to discover your true parentage. It must be a shock for him, too.'

'Well, George is a lovely man. It may be a nice shock.'

'I hope so, for his sake.' Magda gave herself a shake. 'Can I get you another cup of tea?'

'No thanks, I need to go. Is that all, Magda? You look as if there's something more.'

'No, that's it.' Magda had revealed enough confidences today already, ones that weren't hers to reveal. But she had no intention of revealing the one closest to her heart, the one she kept hidden even from herself.

Ten

George wondered if he was doing the right thing or about to open a can of worms best left undisturbed. The young New Zealander had sounded very insistent they meet, but what if it was all in his imagination? Though why someone would imagine George might be his father was difficult to believe. He was – had been – a small town solicitor. It wasn't as if there would be anything to inherit when he passed away, something he had no intention of doing for many years to come. And for it to happen just as he was trying to figure out how to approach Magda with…

But there could be no prospect of that now, not till this was settled. His mind went around and around in circles all the way to the capital. By the time he reached the outskirts of the city he'd almost convinced himself the man was mistaken. He'd meet with him, listen politely to what he had to say, perhaps treat himself to lunch at the National Gallery, then return home and let Magda know it had all been a furphy.

As soon as he saw the man seated in the foyer, his thick auburn hair almost the exact colour of Rose's, his face a younger version of the one George saw in the mirror every morning, George knew he'd been wrong. If this wasn't his son, his and Rose's, then he must have a double over there in New Zealand.

The man rose as George approached. He held out his hand. 'I'm Guy Howard, and you must be…'

'George, George Turnbull.' George took his outstretched hand in his, noting the firm grip. He didn't know what to say.

'This must be a shock.' Guy pushed back a lock of hair that was threatening to fall over his forehead.

George had one exactly the same. He nodded.

'It was a shock to me too. But I guess I've had a few weeks to take it in. Why don't we grab a cup of tea – or would you prefer coffee?' He gestured to the café which adjoined the hotel foyer.

'Coffee would be good.' Strong black coffee was exactly what George needed to cope with the sight of this man, who must indeed be the son he hadn't known existed.

'I'll get it.' Guy headed to the counter while George collapsed into a bench seat by the window. Watching the tall young man – who must be fifty – was like seeing himself. It was an odd feeling, as if he was in two places, in two times periods, at once. Was this how other parents felt? He was a parent. He had a son. The word sat strangely on his lips as he tried it out for size. At least Guy hadn't called him Dad. But what if he had, if he did?

'Here you are.'

He was back and placed two matching mugs of black coffee on the table before taking a seat opposite George. 'I look like you,' he said, breaking the silence.

George nodded again. He couldn't argue with that. 'How did you learn about me?' He was curious. It had been fifty years. Had Rose kept her silence all that time?

Guy took a long drink of coffee before replying. He wasn't finding this easy either. He didn't reply immediately. Instead he said, 'I had to come to Canberra for a conference. A medical conference. I'm a paediatrician in Wellington.'

A doctor. He'd done well for himself then. Rose must be proud. 'Your mother,' he prompted.

'That's why I'm here. As I think I said, she passed away last month. It was when I was going through her things… I had no idea…' He ran a hand through his hair. 'I thought my mum and dad…'

George sipped his coffee and waited. Guy was like him. He'd get his story out in his own good time.

'Anyway,' Guy looked up to meet George's eyes, 'I found letters… from you.'

The letters Rose never answered. She kept them?

'It was the dates that got me thinking. Dad died several years ago – cancer – so I couldn't ask him. It's his name on my birth certificate, but the dates on the letters… He must have known. She must have been pregnant before you wrote them, before she came back to New Zealand.'

'Before she met your dad?'

'No. They grew up together. I thought they'd always been a couple. She never gave any indication… Hell,' he raked his hair again, 'I'm not doing this very well.'

George decided to help him. 'I think what you're trying to say is that you discovered your mother and I had an affair when she was over here at uni, and you've worked out the man you knew as your dad couldn't have been.'

'Precisely.' Guy took a gulp of coffee.

George watched him as he drank. He was a son to be proud of, but what right did he have? And he didn't have the answers to the questions that had interrupted his sleep all those years ago, almost cost him his degree. Why didn't Rose answer his letters? Had she always been in love with this man, this childhood sweetheart? Had George only been a student fling? Whoever he'd been – this man who'd taken his place – he must have known. George wasn't sure whether he admired his devotion or despised his duplicity.

'Your father?'

'He was a good dad, the best.' Guy looked down into his mug, embarrassed. 'His name was Allen, Allen Howard. I always thought… I looked up to him. I was devastated when he died. Mum was, too.'

George didn't speak. There was nothing he could say. He looked across the table again, the realisation gradually dawning on him. This man was his son, the son he'd been denied. A flood of resentment flowed through him. How dare Rose deprive him of the opportunity to know his own child. He'd wanted to marry her. She knew that. All those lost years. He felt a tear come to his eye. And, for some reason, he thought of Magda.

They talked more before Guy finally and regretfully left, promising to keep in touch. Then George went, as he'd planned, to the National Gallery. But he was confused. He couldn't stop thinking about Guy and what he'd said about wanting George to meet his wife and son.

This wasn't only about the man he'd just met, the man who he now knew to be his son. This was about a whole new family.

His lunch tasted like sawdust and the paintings – even his favourite Ned Kelly series – failed to evoke the patriotic feelings they usually did.

He turned, left and drove home, feeling more confused than ever. He needed to talk to Magda.

Eleven

The call from George came late afternoon. Magda had been expecting it. She knew George so well; knew how he'd be feeling after meeting his son for the first time.

'Can I drop by, Magda? I think I need an infusion of your wise counsel.'

'Of course, George. You know you're welcome any time. You'll stay to dinner?'

There was a pause, and she could almost see him debating the wisdom of dinner.

'I won't take no for an answer,' she said, trying to inject a cheerful note into her voice. She could hear from his tone he was struggling.

People got themselves into such a tangle – Sally, Pia and now George. She heard it all the time from her massage clients and those young women – and some not so young – who came to her to have their tealeaves read. She always laughed and said, 'You'd think it was true' but she knew that most of the time it was.

She prepared a vegetable lasagne and was just popping it into the oven when Caesar and Brutus stirred from their spots and bounded towards the door. Their hearing was sharper than hers these days. When she looked out, George's car was making its way up the driveway from the gate. Magda gave her hands a quick rinse and wiped down the benchtop before going to the door to greet him.

*

'So, how did it go?'

The lasagne was cooking away, the dogs had been fed and watered, George had accompanied her out to ensure all was well with the horses, and they were relaxing in the sunroom with glasses of merlot.

George took a gulp of wine, then twirled the glass in his hands before replying. 'He's definitely my son,' he said at last. 'The image of me at his age, apart from the hair. He has Rose's hair.'

Magda smiled inwardly. She'd been right. But George was sitting limply. He was blinking rapidly.

'It must have been a shock.'

George nodded.

'And he'd just found out, too?'

He nodded again.

'So, what's he like?' Magda decided the best thing to do was to get George to talk about it, talk about him.

'He's a fine-looking man.'

'He would be, if he looks like you.'

George's face broke into the semblance of a smile.

That was better.

'He's here for a medical conference. He's a paediatrician. He's done well for himself.'

'And why wouldn't he? He's your son.' Magda couldn't understand why George was being so diffident.

'I guess so.' He sighed and took another drink of wine. 'It's such a waste, Magda. All those lost years – years when I could have…' He shook his head.

'I know. But you can't turn back time. Think of the future. Does he have a family? Did he tell you much about himself?'

George seemed to rouse himself and become more animated. 'Yes. He's married. Her name is Anita, and there's a son – my grandson.' There was a note of wonder in his voice.

'A grandson? Oh, George!' Magda was tempted to hug him but resisted the urge. A hug from her might not be welcome right now.

'Oliver,' George said, almost to himself. 'Oliver Howard.'

Magda was saved from replying by the ping from the oven letting her know the lasagne was cooked. 'I need to get that.' She rose to go into the kitchen, George following.

It seemed George didn't want to say any more about his newly found family, so over dinner Magda talked about her day. She recounted how Pia had been her first massage client, her tea with Jo, finishing with, 'I always seem to be the one handing out advice.' She conveniently omitted the worry she'd shared with Jo. But she had the distinct impression George wasn't listening. His mind was elsewhere. This was unusual enough for her to comment.

'George, did you hear anything I've said?'

'Sorry, Magda. I can't stop thinking about this afternoon. I can hardly believe it happened. I have a son, and a grandson. He wants me to meet them – his wife and son. Imagine that?'

'That sounds wonderful.' Magda tried to share his enthusiasm, but part of her was sad. George was her friend, her best friend. He'd been there for her ever since Bill died. He had no family. She and her boys had been his family. Now he had found this Guy and Oliver, where would that leave her? She felt a trace of fear, fear at the threat of a loneliness she'd never had to experience. It was foolish, she knew. She had her own family, and they'd be with her for Christmas. And George wasn't her only friend. She had lots of friends. But his news brought home to her how important George's friendship was to her, how much she relied on him to be part of her life.

But George was still absorbed in thoughts of his new family and those lost years. 'How could she do it to me, Magda? Rose? To think that... I loved her, I thought she loved me too. All those years, I've been wrong. What a fool, a stupid fool.'

'I'm sorry, but you weren't to know. You were both so young. She's the fool for...'

'I don't want your pity!' George turned away. 'I have to go.' He stood up and left.

Magda listened to the door close, to his car start up, the sound of the engine fading into the distance and felt her eyes moisten. She knew she should be happy for him, happy he had discovered his family. Why did it feel like she'd lost her friend?

Twelve

Three weeks had passed since George met Guy. In that time, Guy had emailed several times, sending photos of himself, Anita, and Oliver. He'd shown George photos of his wife and son on his iPhone when they met, but George had been too flustered to take much note. Now, at home, he was able to pore over them to his heart's content.

And pore over them he did. Young Oliver was nothing like his dad – or George. He must take after his mother's family, with the same thick blond hair, prominent nose and cleft in his chin as Anita. She'd written to him, too, telling him how, although stunned at first, Guy was coming to terms with having found him and was talking about organising a family trip to Australia – to Granite Springs.

It seemed his grandson found the whole situation amusing and had difficulty in believing the conservative, motherly woman he knew as his grandma had been so flighty as to have an affair when she was a student, and his dad was the result. George chuckled when he read that. The Rose they knew and loved was a very different Rose to the feisty, flirtatious girl he'd fallen in love with.

Today they'd planned a Skype call, and he was nervous. It was one thing to have met Guy in Canberra, to communicate by email, but to see all three of them live on Skype was another matter. Magda had asked if he wanted her to be there – in the background – to give him support, but he'd declined her offer. He had arranged for them to meet afterwards for dinner at the local Italian restaurant, thinking he might well need her reassuring presence after what he was sure was going to be an ordeal.

In the event, it was anything but. First, he saw Guy's familiar face on the screen.

'Good to see you again, George,' he said. 'I've thought about you a lot. And I went through Mother's things again. I found some old photos, from when she was in Sydney. I think I recognise you in a few of them, along with a crowd of other people. It was like looking at myself as a student – weird.'

George chuckled. 'Now you know how I felt when I saw you.'

They chatted for a few minutes before a lovely blonde woman George recognised as Anita popped her head next to Guy's.

'Hello, George,' she said, smiling. 'I'm so glad to see you. I won't take up Guy's time with you now, but I'm looking forward to meeting you properly. Guy will fill you in.' She blew him a kiss and disappeared.

She was gone before he could ask what she meant. George felt a warm glow fill him. It was such a relief to know they welcomed his presence in what was clearly a close-knit family.

'Anita's let the cat out of the bag,' Guy said with a grin. 'If you're agreeable, we'd like to come to Granite Springs to visit you over Christmas. Neither of us have any family here now, and we thought...'

George felt his eyes prickle.

'What do you say?'

'Hey, Grandad. Is it okay to call you that?' A cheerful young face surrounded by a mop of blond hair pushed in front of Guy's. 'I'm really looking forward to Christmas. I've never been to Australia.'

George laughed. This must be Oliver. He was a good-looking young man.

'Sorry, George. We're all excited to meet you. Now, about Christmas. Just say if it's not convenient. But we'll need to book our flights – and accommodation.'

'No, I mean, yes.' George laughed again. 'It will be lovely to see you all, and Christmas will be perfect. But there's no need to book accommodation. I have plenty of room here. You can stay with me. And I'd love it if you called me Grandad, Oliver. I never thought I'd have a grandson.'

By the time George closed down the computer he was feeling better, though it was still hard to believe the three people he'd been speaking with were his family. He checked his watch. There was still an hour or so before he was to meet Magda. He went to the study where he knew there was a box of old photos. He pulled out the box and raked through them till he found what he was looking for. There were his copies of the shots Guy must have been talking about. He was with Rose and four others whose names he couldn't recall, and there was another of Rose and him in their glad rags ready for some ball or other. He smiled at the memories they evoked. But there was no rush of emotion. It had all been a long time ago, another lifetime. He was a different person now. He packed them up again without regret and prepared for dinner with Magda.

*

The restaurant was a hive of activity and the delicious aroma of garlic and herbs greeted George as he pushed open the door, making him realise he was hungry. He'd been so strung up about the call from Guy that he'd barely eaten since breakfast.

'Evening, Mr Turnbull,' the waiter greeted him. 'Dining alone tonight?' George was a regular here, usually eating on his own.

'Table for two tonight, Tony. I did make a booking.'

'So you did.' Tony checked the bookings. 'Sorry. Let me show you to your table.' He led George to a secluded spot towards the back of the restaurant.

George ordered a bottle of merlot which he knew Magda would enjoy and settled back in his seat. People-watching was a favourite pastime of his, one he often indulged in when eating alone. He'd discovered you could tell a lot about people by watching how they interacted in a restaurant, both with each other and with the staff. It had served him well over the years when he was practicing law; it had helped him understand what made his clients tick.

But tonight, his mind was focussed on seeing Magda. He was eager to share his news with her, the news that his new family would be here for Christmas. Maybe they could plan something together, not on Christmas day, of course, but perhaps on Christmas Eve or Boxing Day. Guy hadn't said how long they intended to stay, but surely it would be for a few days, maybe a week. It would be wonderful if they could arrive before Christmas and attend the performance of the Messiah. Although he'd no longer be conducting the performance this year, Owen had made sure he was involved, and his contribution would be recorded in the program.

He was basking in feelings of satisfaction with his life, when the door opened and Magda walked in. Though to say she walked in, in no way described her entrance. Everywhere she went, Magda brought with her a sense of something intangible, a presence which was difficult to describe. Although small in stature, Magda had a way of becoming the centre of attention.

Catching sight of George, her face lit up, and George felt his heart leap, all thoughts of Rose and his past forgotten in the delight of seeing her. He stood to greet her with a peck on the cheek. 'How are you, my dear?'

'I'm very well, George. But what about you? How was your call? I've been thinking of you – sending positive vibes your way. Thanks,' she added to the waiter who arrived at that point with the wine, and George indicated he should pour both glasses, forgoing the customary tasting.

'Well, your positive vibes seem to have worked. It was a good call. But let's order first, then I'll tell you all about it.'

'Lovely.' Magda picked up her menu, then laid it down again. 'I don't know why I even bother looking, I always order the same here. I'll have the eggplant parmigiana. You?'

'I can never go past the Pavarotti gnocchi. We're creatures of habit.'

George placed their orders and gazed across at his companion, Magda was looking particularly lovely tonight. She was wearing a dusky pink top and had thrown one of those pashmina things in a dull grey across her shoulders. The combination set off her silver hair to perfection. She was a beauty. He lowered his eyes, unwilling for her to see his admiration. He didn't want to frighten her off. But hadn't that been the problem all the years he'd known her? Maybe it was time to come clean about his feelings.

'Now.' Magda folded her arms on the table and leant forward. 'Your call.'

George picked up his glass and took a sip before replying. 'As I said, it went well. I had a good chat with Guy. Anita – his wife – popped her head in to say hello, and I met Oliver, my grandson.' George knew his voice took on a special note when he uttered Oliver's name. 'He asked if he could call me Grandad. It brought a tear to my eye. Grandad.' He savoured the word. 'I never thought I'd have someone call me that.'

'Oh, George!' Magda put her hand on his, her eyes misting over.

'And the big news is they're coming here for Christmas – to Granite Springs.' He beamed.

'Oh, George,' Magda repeated. 'That's… wonderful.'

But George sensed her hesitation, the fact her tone didn't match her words. What was wrong? Wasn't she pleased for him?

'I know you invited me to join you and your family,' he said, it suddenly occurring to him why she might be upset. 'But that was before…' he drew in his breath, '…I had my own family coming to visit.' He turned his hand to clasp hers, then released it as their meals arrived. 'I'm sorry to upset your plans, Magda, but you must see…'

'Of course.' She made a play of unfolding her napkin, her eyes lowered.

'I thought we might all get together when they're here. You're my oldest friend. I'd like you to meet them. Maybe on Christmas Eve or Boxing Day or… I'm hoping they'll be here in time for the performance of the Messiah. Owen's been good at involving me this year, as I think I said.'

'Sounds good. I'll look forward to it.'

They chatted as they ate, but George was conscious Magda was feeling slighted in some way. He couldn't understand it. He wanted to talk more about Guy, Anita and Oliver, share his excitement, arrange to let her see the photographs so she could wonder at the family likeness. But he did none of those things.

It wasn't till he was walking home, Magda having driven off in her little blue ute, that it occurred to him why she might be feeling rejected. He'd been part of Magda's Christmas Day every year, ever since she and Bill were married. First Bill, then Magda had included him as part of their family, made him feel welcome, ensured he didn't spend the festive season alone. Until this year, when he'd told her he was going to spend it with his own newfound family.

Thirteen

Magda wasn't sure why she felt upset as she drove home through the darkness. She should be happy for George, happy he'd discovered a family he didn't know he had, happy they were joining him for Christmas. But instead, there was an aching void somewhere inside, an ache that wouldn't go away, that stayed with her for the entire trip home to Halcyon, refusing to leave her in peace.

Inside the house, she was greeted by the dogs, and fussing over them and letting them out for a run kept her occupied for several minutes. But when they were back inside and settling down for the night, her spirits dropped again.

Making herself a mug of hot chocolate, Magda tried to figure out what was wrong. It was only as she struggled to settle in her favourite chair and found it difficult to get comfortable the realisation hit her. She was jealous, jealous of the family that was taking over her friend's life. How stupid was that?

In an attempt to distract herself, she turned on the television. But as she flicked through the channels, nothing appealed to her. Instead, she tuned into the radio, finding a programme of chamber music to soothe her. But that didn't work either. The piece was one which she and George had often listened to together. It brought back all those times they'd spent, evenings in her old house or his, chatting, listening to music, sharing their thoughts and worries.

It was no good. Magda knew she was being selfish. She had no claim on George. He deserved this chance at happiness, a chance to connect with a son and grandson he never knew he had. She had her own sons, her own grandchildren. How could she want to deny him the same happiness?

She finished her drink and headed for bed. But even there, thoughts of George broke into her dreams.

*

Next morning, Magda felt better as she set off for her walk with Caesar and Brutus. Oblivious of their mistress's disturbed night, they were full of energy and eager to check out all the new smells along the way. They never failed to make her smile at their antics as they tussled with each other; each trying to outdo the other in their attempts to be the first to discover what had changed since their last inspection of the grassy areas on the edges of the lane.

'Morning, Magda,' Owen Larsen hailed her from where he was laying out pellets for his goats.

'Morning, Owen.' Magda moved closer to the fence, wary of touching it as she knew it was electrified – a sensible measure to ensure the animals were safe and didn't attempt to escape. 'How're things?'

'All good here.' He walked across to the fence line. 'We haven't seen you around lately. Hope all is well with you, too. Did you know Pia has moved into town? We miss her and the little one, but it's good for her to have some independence. I'm glad she decided to stay in Granite Springs.'

'I've been busy settling back in and getting my business up and running again. Pia was my first client. She did mention something about moving to town – to Sally Anderson's place?'

'Wow, I can't tell you anything. Fran did say you always know what's going to happen before it actually does.'

'Not always.' But Magda grinned. 'But I hear you've co-opted George Turnbull into your choir rehearsals.' George was still on Magda's mind and she knew how pleased he was to be included in the preparations for this year's performance of the Messiah.

'He's a good man, and a hard act to follow. You and he are friends, aren't you?' He gazed at her with what she imagined was more than casual curiosity.

To her annoyance, Magda felt herself redden. She didn't embarrass easily, but somehow this question asked so casually brought a blush to her cheeks. She put a hand up to her face in an attempt to suppress it. But Owen hadn't noticed.

'Why don't you come to dinner one of these nights? I feel I hardly know you, and Fran speaks highly of you. I'll get her to call you, shall I?'

'That would be lovely. Now, I'd better get on.' Her dogs were becoming restless, edging towards her feet to remind her this was supposed to be a walk, not a talkfest. 'Give my regards to Fran.'

'I will.' Owen turned back to his goats, and Magda walked on, realising she hadn't responded to his question about George. Why had she been embarrassed, too embarrassed to answer? She and George were friends, always had been. Nothing had changed. But, Magda realised, *she* had changed. It had been her year away that did it. She'd missed her old friend more – much more – than she anticipated. If she was honest with herself, it wasn't only the town of Granite Springs that had drawn her back, nor was it her dogs and horses, though they were important to her. The main drawcard had been her old friend, George Turnbull.

Fourteen

It felt as if he'd never been away. George had been attending the choir rehearsals for several weeks now and the experience never failed to delight him. When Owen first approached him, he'd thought it would mean attending one rehearsal, maybe two. But he was wrong. The younger man welcomed his attendance – and input – and assured him he wanted him there right up till the performance on the Saturday before Christmas. Although no longer conducting the choir, George felt his spirits lift each time he walked into a rehearsal.

Tonight was no different. He was running late, and Owen had already called the group to order when he slipped through the door. He took his customary seat, prepared to enjoy the evening. But something was wrong. It had been bothering him all day. It was Magda; their dinner last night. It hadn't gone as he expected. He'd arrived full of enthusiasm after his New Zealand call, eager to share his news with his old friend, his best friend. But… Magda hadn't reacted with her usual pleasure at his news. Her reaction had been lukewarm to put it mildly.

He tried to put Magda out of his mind and concentrate on the glorious sounds of the choristers, appreciate how Owen was urging them to greater and greater heights. He was a far better conductor than George had been. But it was no use. He shouldn't have come. But if he hadn't, what would he have done? He'd have spent the evening moping around the house, unable to settle there, either.

'All good?'

He looked up to see Owen gazing at him, his face full of concern. He hadn't even been aware the music had stopped. 'Fine, son. Just thinking.'

'Okay. By the way, Fran and I would like you to come to dinner. Friday okay with you? I'm cooking. You haven't lived till you've tried my Spanish paella.'

'I…' George wasn't sure he wanted to go out there, so close to Magda's place. He'd never felt so insecure about her before. But Owen didn't give him time to refuse.

'Seven o'clock,' he said, before turning back to the choir and continuing the rehearsal.

*

By the time Friday came around, George still hadn't heard from Magda. This was unusual. Normally, hardly a day went by without one of them calling or texting the other. He must have really offended her. And now he was obligated to going to dinner with Owen and Fran.

For most of the day, while he was searching on the Ancestry website, trying to discover links to his great-grandparents who emigrated to Australia in their early twenties, the image of Magda kept insinuating itself between him and the screen. Finally, he could stand it no longer. He had as much right to contact Magda as she had to contact him. What had he been waiting for? Why hadn't he picked up the phone before now? He knew why. There had been a sense of unease, a hint of something he didn't associate with Magda. It had been when he mentioned Guy and his family coming to Granite Springs for Christmas. Magda had gone very quiet. His great news, the news he'd been so eager to share with her had touched a nerve in his friend and something had shifted in their relationship.

He picked up the phone, hesitating before pressing direct dial, determined to do whatever it took, apologising if necessary, to regain her good opinion. The only thing he wasn't able to do was to make his new family disappear, or to prevent their visiting him for Christmas. The phone rang and rang, but there was no reply, only the disembodied voice of the answer machine. He hung up without leaving a message.

*

Magda returned from a long walk, reaching home as the answer phone clicked in. But there was no message. She shrugged. If it was important, they'd ring back. She busied herself ensuring the dogs had food and water, then headed out to the paddock to check on the horses, waving when she saw Owen in the distance checking on his goats.

Back inside, she made herself a cup of peppermint tea before going to shower and change. It was kind of Fran to have invited her to dinner. Over tea, after Fran's weekly massage on Wednesday, the younger woman had reiterated Owen's invitation and tonight was the agreed date. Towelling her hair dry after the shower, Magda debated what to wear, settling on a pair of grey linen pants topped with a long-sleeved shirt in her favourite royal blue. Fran and Owen were a casual couple so there was no need to dress up, and those old ranch-style houses could be chilly, even at this time of year.

It was time to go. Instructing Caesar and Brutus to stay, leaving the outside lights on, and ensuring she had her torch in her bag, Magda set off. Although it was still light, she knew it would be dark when she made her way home and didn't intend walking up the lane with only the stars to guide her.

As she trudged up the driveway to Fran's house, Magda heard a car behind her. Turning, she recognised George's white Prius moving slowly towards her. She stepped off the path to allow him to pass, receiving a wave from him as she did so. What was George doing here?

It was obvious. He'd been invited to dinner, too. Magda was tempted to turn back, but she could already see Fran waiting to greet her. It was too late for a change of heart.

She reached the house just as George was stepping out of his car. He greeted her as usual with a hug and a peck on the cheek. It was lovely to feel his arms around her again, his firm bulk against her, his lips on her cheek.

'Good to see you, Magda. I didn't expect you to be here, too. I tried to call you today. Are we good?'

'We're good.' How could she have been so stupid as to feel jealous? His must have been the call she missed. But why hadn't he left a message?

'Hey, you two!' Fran's voice broke through.

Magda and George drew apart to see Fran gazing at them indulgently. *She didn't think? My God, maybe she did!*

'Fran. I didn't realise you'd invited George, too.'

'Owen did. It's good to see you both together.'

They followed her into the large family kitchen which was fragrant with a delightful herb and spicy aroma. A large pan was bubbling away on the stove and a black cat was lying on a rocking chair beside it. It looked up curiously when they walked in then closed its eyes again.

Owen appeared, gave Magda a peck on the cheek and shook George's hand. 'Glad you both could make it. Come through and I'll get you a drink. What'll you have, Magda? White wine okay? Can you get Magda a glass, Fran?' he asked, without waiting for a reply. 'Now, George, I want you to try a nip from a bottle of *Laphroaig* I picked up. The local bottle shop had a special deal on it. I'd like your opinion.'

Fran rolled her eyes at Magda and opened the fridge to pour two glasses of white wine, while George and Owen debated the relative merits of *Laphroaig* and *Glenfiddich*. 'I thought we'd eat in here tonight. It's cosier. If that's okay with you?' She gestured to the large wooden table set for four.

'Now,' Fran instructed Owen, when the two men had reached an agreement on the whisky, 'I don't want you to spend the evening discussing music with George. I'm sure we can all find something more interesting to talk about.'

'More interesting than music?' Owen raised one eyebrow, then grinned. 'I'm sure Magda would be interested to hear how…'

'Enough!' Fran covered her ears. But she was grinning too. 'See what I have to put up with, Magda?'

But Magda could see Fran was joking from the way she looked at Owen, from the way they touched each other when they thought no one was looking. 'George told me you're making a few changes to the Christmas performance of the Messiah this year,' she said to Owen.

'Just a few. George has been kind enough to lend me his wisdom, accumulated over his many years with the choristers. Isn't that right, George?'

George pulled at his collar. 'Well, I hope I've been of some help, and it's been good to be involved again. But less of the *many years*. It makes me sound like Methuselah.' He chuckled, but Magda sensed his underlying irritation.

'George and I may be older than you pair, but we don't like to be reminded of it. We still feel like spring chickens inside, and there's nothing worse than being reminded of how the years have passed. I get enough of that from my children.' Magda laughed to take the sting out of her words, then blanched remembering how cool she'd been to George about his son's appearance. Deciding to rectify it, she added, 'Speaking of children, George has some exciting news.'

Both Fran and Owen turned to George who squirmed in his chair. *Damn, had she put her foot in it again?*

There was the sound of a timer going off, giving George – and Magda – a reprieve.

'Back in a tick.' Owen rose to take the paella off the stove and, several minutes later, they were all served with steaming bowls of paella along with green salad and crusty bread.

'Now,' Owen said, when he joined them again, 'what's this exciting news, George?'

Magda winced. 'Perhaps I shouldn't have mentioned it.'

'No, no, Magda. Everyone will know soon enough. And it's not as if I'm ashamed of it. I've recently discovered I have a son. He's been living in New Zealand and I knew nothing about him.'

Magda saw Fran flinch. She wished she hadn't brought it up. In her desire to redress things with George, she'd overlooked Fran's own disappointment, the child she'd lost and her inability to have others.

But Fran swiftly recovered. 'Sounds interesting, George. Tell us more.'

The meal progressed slowly as George recounted the arrival of Guy in his life and the news his new family would be spending Christmas with him.

'How wonderful. It's like a fairy story,' Fran said wistfully when he finished.

'Mmm,' George looked across at Magda.

She gave him what she hoped was an encouraging smile. 'Isn't it?' she asked. 'I'm looking forward to meeting them,' she said, trying to sound as if she meant it.

'Does he resemble you at all?' Fran asked.

'Spitting image – apart from the hair. He has his mother's hair.' There was a hint of pride in George's voice, one Magda realised she'd failed to notice when they last spoke. She'd been too eaten up with her own jealousy.

'When will they get here? It'd be great if they were here for the Messiah.' It was Owen who spoke, leading to another eyeroll from Fran.

'That's all I hear about these days,' she said with a mock sigh. 'That and the students' Christmas show. They're putting on an old-fashioned pantomime – a modern version of Cinderella.'

'Should be a lot of fun.' Owen picked up their empty plates and bowls. 'Anyone for dessert? Fran has made a delicious apple pie, and I think there's some ice cream.'

'It's only natural for Owen to be caught up in the performances,' Magda said in an attempt to reassure Fran. She remembered how, in previous years, George had confided his worries about the production to her. It was an important event in Granite Springs, one which attracted a huge following, signifying for many the start of the Christmas festivities. It was almost as important as the lighting of the Christmas tree in the centre of town which took place at the beginning of December each year.

'Oh, I know. I'm not complaining. I'm a member of the choir and I'm involved in the uni production too. We rehash both of those in the car on the way home from rehearsals. It's just that I'd rather leave all of it behind when we reach home, but you know Owen.' She spread her hands. 'He's incorrigible. I guess that's one of the reasons I love him.'

Magda felt a lump come to her throat. These two were so obviously happy together, so right for each other. She glanced at George, sitting opposite apparently lost in his thoughts while Owen fetched the dessert, then at the cat who suddenly stretched and yawned before settling down again. What would it be like to be in a relationship again? How would she feel to lose her independence, to be subject to the demands of another person, to…?

Just then, George met her eyes and she dropped hers, as if he'd be able to read her thoughts in them.

As Magda predicted, it was dark when she and George left. She refused his offer of a lift saying she could still find her own way home, but smiled as she did, and added, 'I hope I'll see you again soon, George,' and gave him the hug with which they normally parted. She could see Owen and Fran smiling at them indulgently again as they waved them off. This time she didn't care.

65

Fifteen

The dinner with Owen and Fran seemed to mark a turning point for Magda and George. Neither mentioned it, but they renewed the frequency of their former communications, and Magda agreed to look at the photos he was so eager to share with her.

It was a lovely summer evening. Magda was singing to herself as she checked the horses, a red headband keeping her silver curls out of her eyes. She knew George would laugh to see her like this, in her old tee-shirt and floral dungarees – the ones her granddaughter had insisted she buy from a market stall. 'They're so you,' Holly exclaimed when she picked them up. 'You're not like any other grandma I know.' It was praise indeed, coming from the nineteen-year-old, and Magda had worn them frequently around the house, garden and horse paddock since her return. She'd even managed to take a selfie to send to Holly to show her wearing them, surrounded by her animals.

Tonight, George had invited her to a homecooked dinner and promised not to bore her too much with the photos of Guy and his family. Magda had steeled herself to maintain a positive attitude and to avoid becoming annoyed or resentful at what would no doubt be George's excitement as he showed off his new family.

Changing into a pair of clean and pressed jeans and a short-sleeved cotton top, Magda fed the dogs before leaving. As she drove into town, she reflected, not for the first time, how odd it must be to be presented with a family fully grown, to have missed out on all the fun early stages of both his son and grandson, and to have to get to know them as adults.

Magda thought back to the enjoyable times she'd had with her own brood – times which George had shared with her – and knew she'd have hated to miss those formative years. What must it be like for George who had to rely on photos to fill in the gaps? Then her thoughts went to the woman who'd hidden her pregnancy from George, kept him in ignorance of his son, married another man.

What kind of woman would do that? What had Rose really been like? According to George, she'd been lovely, bright, and had, he thought, loved him. Had he been wrong? Had she always had her old flame tucked away back home waiting for her? Or had she taken the easy way out when she discovered she was pregnant, married the old friend to satisfy her parents, to enable her to stay with them in New Zealand?

They'd probably never know. And maybe George didn't care. But Magda would love to find out what prompted such an act of betrayal. And what of the man she had married, the man Guy called his dad, grew up thinking was his dad? Did he know Guy wasn't his son? Had she fooled him, too? Did he love her so much he was willing to accept a child fathered by another? Magda knew some men did.

It was a bag of conundrums and try as she might, Magda couldn't work it out. While she was adept at foretelling the future and had experienced a strong sense of Rose when she was with George – before he heard from Guy – she had no insight into the past.

She was still pondering over it when she drew up outside George's home. Like many of the older houses in Granite Springs, it was a red brick federation-style home with the typical elaborate gables, timber features, dominant roofline, and leadlight windows. The house had originally belonged to George's parents and he had taken good care of it over the years. The front garden showed evidence of recent care, and the windows were sparkling.

For the first time, it occurred to Magda her old friend might be lonely. Since he'd retired, first from his legal practice, then from the choir, perhaps time hung heavy on his hands. She wondered how she could help.

The door flew open almost before she locked the car, George's familiar craggy face breaking into a smile at the sight of her.

'Come in, come in,' he said, giving her the usual hug and peck on the cheek. As she followed him into the house, through the hallway and into the family kitchen, Magda wondered how it would feel to have a different sort of relationship with him – closer, more intimate. Sitting at the kitchen table, she watched him taking a bottle of wine from the fridge and filling two glasses with the chilled semillon blanc, noticed his large hands, his broad shoulders, his strong neck, his still thick white hair – unusual for a man of his age – and felt her heart beat faster, an unfamiliar tingle in her limbs.

'Okay?' George turned to hand her a glass.

Magda almost choked, hoping he couldn't read her mind. But why would he? She was the one gifted with second sight. George was just… just George, good old George. But, suddenly, he wasn't good old George any longer. It was as if she was seeing a stranger, a stranger who she had a strong desire to touch, to be touched by, to… She took a gulp of wine and hid her face in the glass. 'Thanks, George.'

'I've put together a chicken parmigiana. Saw one of those TV chefs do it on the box and thought I'd have a go. And there's a green salad to go with it. I know you don't often eat meat…' His voice trailed off.

'That'll be lovely, George. I do eat chicken from time to time, and fish. It's just red meat I tend to avoid.'

'Good-oh!' He joined her at the table and reached for his iPad. 'Dinner will take a little while. Would you like to look at the photos Guy sent while we're waiting?'

Magda swallowed. This was why she was here, after all. 'Sure,' she said, pivoting around in her seat to get a better view.

For the next twenty minutes or so, Magda dutifully admired the photos showing a younger version of George, a smiling blonde woman, and a teenager with his mother's blond good looks and just a hint of George and his father in his posture. 'They look lovely,' she said honestly. 'You must be proud.'

'I am.' George pulled on one ear. 'But I'd still like to know…'

'Rose?'

'Yes. Why… why she chose to cut me out, to marry this other man. We were close. But, I guess… Maybe she wanted to go back to New Zealand. I never lied about my intention to set up in practice back here in Granite Springs. It's always been home to me.'

'Perhaps she felt the same way about her home town.' Magda

tried to put herself in Rose's position – home from uni, a sick mother, pregnant by a man who lived in another country, who had no idea of her situation, who had his own plans. Then a childhood sweetheart who wanted or was willing to marry her. Maybe she'd have done the same.

'Maybe that's why,' she said, laying a hand on George's shoulder.

He sighed. 'It was all such a long time ago. You're right. I didn't consider her wishes. Since I met Guy, I've been remembering those days, but I've been stuck in thinking about it from my point of view. It must have been awful for her to discover she was carrying my child when her mother was so sick and…' He turned off the iPad and took Magda's hands in his. 'But I can't help wishing she'd told me, given me the opportunity to… I don't know. Maybe I would have gone to New Zealand when I graduated. It's the fact I didn't know – that she didn't give me the chance to do the right thing by her.'

Magda smiled at the old-fashioned term. That was George all over. He was such an old-fashioned guy.

'You would have. I know you would. That's the sort of person you are.' She smiled and squeezed the hands holding hers.

'Then where would we have been?' George's eyes met hers. There was such emotion in them, Magda's breath caught. The sentiments she felt watching him earlier, welled up again, threatening to overwhelm her. Flustered, she withdrew her hands and took another sip of wine. 'How's dinner coming along?' she asked.

George took a few moments to reply, and when he did it was in a gruff voice, quite unlike himself. 'I'll go and see.'

While he was checking the oven, Magda took a few deep breaths. Where had it all come from – the emotion, the ache inside, the longing for his touch? She'd been celibate for years, never felt the need for intimate contact with anyone, satisfied with her own company. And now this – with George?

They made it through the meal talking of generalities – of happenings in Granite Springs, the performance of the Messiah and their respective forthcoming Christmas preparations. Magda offered to share her favourite Christmas recipes with him – the simpler ones, she joked – and promised to be at the Messiah *with bells on* – 'maybe literally,' she said, laughing. It all helped her try to stifle the unfamiliar and unwanted emotions that were battling within her.

She thought she'd succeeded, managed to hide them from George. So it was a shock when, as they parted, standing outside in the darkness, the light from the house sending shadows onto their faces, George's customary hug was tighter than usual and his lips, instead of grazing her cheek, landed on her lips and remained there for what seemed like a long time.

Sixteen

As George watched Magda's blue ute drive away – as bright and sparkling as the lady herself – all he could think was, *you've done it now, George.* It had been automatic. They'd had such a pleasant evening. Magda had seemed to accept Guy and his new family; she'd even sounded sympathetic to Rose's plight, given George more to think about. When she turned to leave, he'd intended to give her a friendly hug as usual and place the customary peck on her cheek. But somehow, the hug had morphed into an embrace, the sensation of her soft, warm body in his arms leading his lips to seek out hers and… He drew a hand through his hair. How was he going to face her again?

But he couldn't regret it. It had been a long time since he'd felt like this, since that ache had flooded his body, since…

He needed to take a cold shower.

Towelling himself dry, George pulled on a pair of old board shorts and went into the study where he poured himself a glass of whisky. He still couldn't believe what he'd done. He'd been so careful over the years not to reveal his inner feelings to Magda. Why had tonight proved different? Had it been her understanding for his failings as a student, her acceptance of his new family, or had it just been the right time?

They weren't getting any younger and, although fit and healthy, there were some days when George felt old age creeping up on him. He didn't want to wait for old Father Time to remind him it was too late. Damn it! He still had a lot to offer a woman, and Magda was the woman he wanted to offer it to, the woman he wanted to spend his remaining days with, however long or short they might be. But was there any chance she felt the same way, or had he blown it completely?

*

He was still undecided next day which he spent partly in his orchid house and partly on his computer. After seeing the old uni photo Guy had sent him, and finding his copy, he decided to put together an album for Guy and Oliver. It took some time, but he enjoyed the process of scanning the relevant photos and researching online before choosing the website to use. He'd be able to have it completed and delivered by Christmas. At least it took his mind off Magda.

But, when he decided he'd done as much as he could for now, and rose from the spot he'd been sitting in all afternoon, George found he had stiffened up after being in the same position for so long. He needed to stretch his legs. Checking the time, he saw it was almost five. A beer would go down well, as would some company.

He freshened up and set off to walk to the club. The walk would loosen up his joints and the club would provide a welcome glass of beer and perhaps the company he was seeking.

The familiar noise of chatter and the sound of the poker machines met him when he walked past the reception desk and into the club. Before he retired, he'd often dropped in for a middy or a schooner on his way home and, more recently, had spent many a lonely evening here.

He went straight to the bar and ordered a glass of his favourite beer – the *James Squire One Fifty Lashes* would go down a treat – before glancing around the room. He expected to see one or more of his acquaintances, perhaps a former colleague enjoying a quiet beer before going home to dinner. But the man who smiled at him and waved him over to the corner table was a surprise. What was Col Ford doing here? Surely he should be home on his acreage doing whatever it was he did with those animals of his.

'Good to see you, George.' Col rose to shake his hand.

'Good to see you too, Col. What brings you into town?'

'I had to pop into the office to clear up a matter that started when I was still working. Jo and I are having dinner at The Riverside, so I decided to drop in here rather than go all the way home just to turn around again.'

'Right.' George took a seat and a sip of beer. It was good to meet his old colleague. They'd remained friends but didn't see each other often. When he'd been invited out to Yarran for Magda's welcome home, it had been the first time he'd seen Col since the Easter picnic races. Thinking of Magda brought a crease to his forehead.

'Something worrying you?'

'No.' George took another mouthful of beer, relishing how the cold liquid helped dispel his concern – but not completely.

'You can tell me.' Col leant forward. 'It'll go no further. My lips are sealed.' He chuckled.

George regarded his companion thoughtfully. Maybe he could – tell Col his worries. After all, Col Ford had formed a relationship in his later life. He and Jo must have been at least sixty when they got together. And no one had suggested either of them were past it. But he and Magda weren't sixty. They were both in their seventies, and it wasn't their ages George was worried about. It was Magda.

'It's Magda,' he said, shaking his head.

'What's she done? Is she in any trouble? I know you two are friends. I often see her walking the dogs and we have a bit of a yarn. She looked okay last time…'

'No.' George shook his head. 'It's not Magda. It's me.'

Col had been lifting his glass to have another drink. He stopped halfway and lowered the glass. 'You? What have *you* been up to?'

George shook his head. He couldn't do this. How had it occurred to him, even for a second, that he could confide his uncertainty about Magda's feelings with anyone?

'Sorry, George. I didn't mean to sound censorial. Of course, I don't think you've been up to anything untoward. But… you and Magda… I… we've always thought… You've always seemed so close. You never considered getting together?'

'That's just it – the trouble. We both know the rumours, have laughed because there was nothing in them. Bill, her late husband, was my best friend. When he died leaving her with two young boys, I stepped in to do what I could. When the boys left, I continued to see Magda, to help out when necessary. There was never any thought of anything else. Not then.'

'But?' Col raised an eyebrow and took another sip of his beer.

'Over the years, my feelings changed. I never said anything. Magda's always been very loyal to Bill's memory. We both have. But when she was gone for so long, I found I missed her – more than I expected. I started to think. We're both getting older. Maybe we should try to make a go of it. But I was afraid to speak. I didn't want to lose what we had – our strong friendship.'

'So what's changed?'

'Last night. We had dinner together, like we've done so often. We were talking about…' He waved his hand dismissively. He had no intention of going into an explanation of discovering he had a son. 'It doesn't matter what we were talking about. But when we parted, instead of giving her a peck on the cheek, we kissed on the lips.'

'And now you don't know what to do or say?'

George nodded, pleased Col seemed to understand his predicament.

'Maybe her feelings have changed too.'

'You think?' George considered that possibility, trying to remember if Magda had returned his kiss. He thought she had. At least, she hadn't drawn away. But perhaps she'd been too shocked to move.

'I'm probably not the one to offer advice when it comes to women, George. I've only known Alice and Jo. But from my experience, it always helps to talk about things. And it's not me you should be talking to, it's Magda. Talking things through certainly worked with Jo and me.' There was a faraway look in Col's eyes that made George feel he was being made privy to a secret.

The pair continued to drink and chat, and no more was said about George's revelation. But as they parted, Col to meet his wife and George to walk back to his lonely house, Col clapped his hand on George's shoulder. 'Good luck, mate,' he said and walked away.

Luck, George thought as he made his way home. *He'd need more than luck*. But perhaps Col knew what he was talking about; perhaps he should speak with Magda.

Seventeen

Had she imagined it? Had George really kissed her? A proper kiss, not one of those pecks on the cheek she was accustomed to receiving. Their lips definitely met – and held. There was no doubt about that.

But was it his intention, or had she invited it? Magda recalled the rush of yearning that flowed through her at his hug, which was more loving than usual. Had it been for her, or a result of the conversation about Rose? And had she turned her head so that, instead of his kiss landing on her cheek, their lips had met? In other words, had it been George's intention to kiss her on the lips, or had she forced him into it?

Magda fretted about it all next morning while she checked the horses, walked the dogs and worked in the garden she was trying to pull back into shape. Although many of her beautiful plants had survived the fire, her vegetable garden and fruit trees had perished in the smoke and the flames.

As she worked, she carried on a conversation in her head, or with Caesar and Brutus when they came into her orbit. But they were of no use; they had no advice to offer. Finally, she made up her mind to forget it. It was done and, whoever had instigated it, she and George had to carry on being friends, whatever form their friendship might take in the future.

She wondered what George was doing today, what he was thinking. Several times she took out her phone to call him, before putting it back into her pocket. By lunchtime, she was a wreck. It was a good job she had a couple of clients booked in for a massage in the afternoon. She always found it relaxing to set others at ease with what they called her *magic hands*. There was nothing magic about them, that wasn't where the magic lay. She merely used the skills she'd learnt. What she'd also learnt over the years was to provide the proper atmosphere, an ambiance in which her clients could relax, forget the cares of their lives and lose themselves in another world, a world of peace and serenity.

It wasn't easy to provide exactly the correct mood, but Magda managed to create it. She'd done it in her old house, and again here in her new massage studio. It wasn't delivered by the room itself – it could be any room in any house. What Magda did, was to provide the lighting, scents and music all designed to lull her clients into a sense of calm and total relaxation. It was her goal for each to leave with enhanced feelings of wellbeing and contentment. And, according to her clients and the amount of repeat business she generated, she was successful.

Today, she was the one in need of those feelings.

After farewelling her first client, Magda was beginning to feel a sense of calm permeate her body. Her own magic was beginning to work, as long as she remained focussed on her massages and managed to put George out of her mind.

'Hello!' Magda heard her next client call from the veranda. How could she have forgotten Jo Ford was coming today? Jo was the one person with whom she'd let down her guard when she discussed George with her after her last massage a month earlier. Jo hadn't mentioned anything about it since. She was considerate and tactful, but she did have a habit of worming confidences out of people – not unlike Magda herself.

The hour passed quickly, neither of them talking, Jo making the occasional groan of pleasure as Magda managed to release a particularly tight knot. When the treatment was finished and Jo sat up slowly again, Magda said, 'Take your time,' as she always did and handed her a glass of water adding, 'Come through when you're ready.'

As usual, she had two cups of her favourite sweetly smelling camomile tea sitting on the table along with slices of a sponge cake she'd made the day before.

'Feeling better?' she asked.

'Much. I feel wonderful. You've worked your magic again.'

Magda smiled. She joined Jo at the table and took a sip of the refreshing tea. But she should have known. A massage with Magda tended to invite confidences, and Jo hadn't forgotten their discussion of the previous month.

'Everything sorted with George now?' she asked, helping herself to a slice of sponge. 'You spoil me, Magda. How am I ever going to lose weight if you keep feeding me delicious treats like this?'

Magda felt herself blush, not something she did often.

Jo peered at her. 'What did I say?'

Magda looked down into her cup, wishing she'd chosen today to break with the habit of years and hadn't offered her neighbour tea. But if she hadn't, Jo would really have known something was wrong, and would have wormed it out of her anyway.

'Is it George? Has something happened? You mentioned a son reappearing. Didn't it work out for him? Is it worrying you? I know how close you two are. But surely he can deal with it?'

Magda felt like weeping. Jo was so kind. She always wanted to help.

'It is George, and it's not his son. They seem to be getting along like a house on fire. It's me, George and me. Oh, Jo, I'm in such a mess!'

'Do you want to talk about it?' Jo clasped her cup in both hands, her eyes filled with concern. 'I completely understand if you don't. But sometimes it helps to talk to someone who isn't involved. I should know. You've often helped me by listening to my tales of woe.'

'Well…' Magda considered, remembering how she'd told Jo about the odd feeling something had changed between her and George. 'He kissed me!'

Jo laughed. She actually laughed.

Magda wished she'd kept quiet, kept the kiss to herself. She hadn't intended to be the butt of Jo's amusement.

'Sorry. I didn't mean… but, Magda, Col and I did more than kiss the first time we got together.' She buttoned her lips. 'Oh, dear. I didn't mean to tell you that. You won't let on to Col, will you?' she gurgled, laughter still not far away. 'What was so special about this kiss and why are you worried about it? It's good, isn't it?'

Magda gazed out the window seeing her horses in the distance and wished she was anywhere but here. 'It wasn't the kiss itself. But

I'm not sure which of us started it and…' She realised how silly this sounded. She wasn't a teenager. She shouldn't be getting herself tied in knots over a kiss – even one from an old friend, one who she'd like to be something more.

'You wanted him to kiss you?'

'Yes.' Magda heard her voice come out in a squeak. Heavens, she even sounded like a silly teenager. 'Yes,' she said more firmly, 'but I didn't think George shared my feelings, I still don't. That's what makes it so difficult. How did you and Col manage?' she asked, curious. She knew Jo had been a good friend to both Col and his late wife before they got together as a couple.

'We talked about it – afterwards. We decided not to rush into anything. We didn't want to spoil a beautiful friendship. I'm guessing you feel the same – about George. All I can suggest is that you do the same.'

'Talk about it?' Magda wondered how she could possibly do that. While she was good at handing out advice, she wasn't so good at taking it, or at talking about her feelings. Neither was George. It was something they both tended to hedge around.

'Thanks,' she said to Jo when she left. But as she turned back into the house, she felt no further forward. She'd bared her inner feelings to Jo to what end? She still had to face George and that kiss was still between them. Maybe she should just ignore it, pretend it hadn't happened.

Eighteen

George worried over Col's advice all the next day, but come Saturday morning he was no further forward in his thinking. What Col said made sense, but how was he going to bring up the subject with Magda? And how could he arrange to see her – or just drop in – with this on his mind?

Determined to concentrate on other matters, he put together his weekly shopping list and set off for the farmers market. It was held each Sunday in the showground. George still referred to it as the farmers market – and that's how it began with local farmers bringing their produce into town. It had evolved over the years. Now it seemed to be a free-for-all, with stalls selling clothes, jewellery, books, and all sorts of other bric-a-brac jostling for space among the original stallholders.

It was George's habit to set out early to snag the best of the fruit and vegetables, thus avoiding the crowds who descended on the market later in the morning intent on finding a bargain. He'd take them home, pack them away, then head out again for a slap-up Sunday breakfast. There weren't many places open on a Sunday morning in Granite Springs, most restaurant and café owners preferring to observe the sabbath or, at least, take a break from the busy working week.

The small bakery close to the river was one he'd come across by accident several years earlier. He'd been wandering aimlessly along the riverside when he noticed the new establishment and, deciding to give it a try, was immediately won over by the freshly baked bread and croissants. Recently, no doubt due to customer demand, they'd set up a few outside tables by the river and added to their menu to serve a cooked breakfast on Sunday mornings.

This morning, George ordered his usual poached egg and smashed avocado on sour dough bread, along with a mug of black coffee, and settled down to browse through the Sunday paper he'd bought along the way. The sun was warm on his back, a group of galahs were fossicking in the grass on the riverbank and a lone family of ducks were swimming past. If this wasn't paradise, it was very close to it.

The ping of his phone alerted him to a text, and he smiled fondly at the photo Oliver had sent of him playing cricket with his local team. He seemed to be a good lad. This was what it was like to have a grandson. It reminded George how much he'd missed of his own son's teenage years. But he'd be able to make that up to some extent with Oliver. He was looking forward to Christmas so much and had begun to think what gifts he might get for them all and how to best prepare for their visit.

He was at a loss where to start. It was a quandary for an old bachelor like himself. He needed advice from someone more familiar with having family to stay and who might have some inkling of what appealed to young people today. From what he read and saw on television, things had changed greatly from when he was their age.

His meal had just arrived, and he was enjoying his first sip of coffee, when he heard a familiar voice coming from inside the establishment.

'I'll have one of your chocolate and almond croissants and a pot of lemon grass and ginger tea,' Magda said, and, before George could blink, his old friend appeared, peering around for a table. She seemed surprised to catch sight of George and almost turned to go back inside, before realising it was too late. Recovering quickly, she made her way to his table. 'May I join you?' she asked and, without waiting for a reply, pulled out a chair and sat down.

'Don't usually see you in town at this time on a Sunday,' George said, noting Magda was looking very pretty in a pale pink sundress which showed off her tanned shoulders. Her hair appeared to be more carefully styled than usual, and she had a scarf tied around it which gave her a youthful look. She was a good-looking woman who could have any man she chose. How could he imagine she might want him? 'What brings you in today?'

'Oh, you know.'

George didn't. Magda normally kept herself busy on her acreage. Between her garden, her horses, and the dogs, she had little time left to drive into town. And certainly not on a Sunday morning. He tipped his head to the side and waited for further explanation. It wasn't forthcoming. He took a mouthful of toast and avocado, then decided that if they weren't to sit here in silence, it was up to him.

'I always come here for breakfast on Sundays – after the markets. It's something I look forward to.' He began to prattle on about the markets, the stallholders, the fresh produce, and was about to run out of conversation when Magda spoke again.

'I came into town to see you.'

'Your tea and croissant, madam.'

Both looked up at the waiter who was carrying a small wooden board containing a pot of tea, a mug, and a flaky croissant.

'Thanks,' Magda said.

George was staring at her, speechless. What did she mean by saying she'd come in to see him? How did she know he'd be here?

'I didn't expect to see you here. I intended to visit you at home. I actually drove past your house. But I got cold feet and decided to have tea first.'

'Well, you've found me. Why did you want to see me?'

'I… last time… Did… Oh, George, this is so difficult. Can we forget that happened? It didn't mean… I value our friendship. I'd hate to spoil what we have because of one unguarded moment.'

George's heart sank. He looked at the remains of his breakfast – the breakfast he'd been looking forward to – and pushed the plate away. His appetite was completely gone. The kiss he'd been so anxious about hadn't meant anything to Magda. But wasn't that what *he* wanted – to continue as if it hadn't happened, to retain their friendship on the same terms as before? The old George would have been relieved and agreed to say no more about it.

But George knew he wasn't that same person any longer. The new George – the George who now had a son and grandson – wasn't a lonely old bachelor dependent on the crumbs from his friend's table for company. He remembered Col's advice – to talk about it with Magda.

'I don't think I can, Magda – forget it, that is. I value our friendship, too. You're my oldest and best friend. I'd hate to lose you. But I have to be honest. I can't say our kiss didn't mean anything to me. It did. It meant a lot. And, if saying that, if wanting to take our friendship in another direction is distasteful to you, then…' He wasn't sure how to continue.

While he'd been speaking, George had been looking down at the table, loath to meet Magda's eyes. Now he looked up to see hers filled with tears. Hell, he hadn't meant to make her cry. 'Don't cry, Magda.' He pulled out a handkerchief and handed it to her.

Magda wiped her eyes – as daintily as she did everything else, then folded the handkerchief carefully. 'Sorry, George. You took me by surprise. I didn't expect… It meant something to me, too, and Jo said…'

Jo? She'd talked about it with Jo? George experienced a spark of annoyance, before remembering his talk with Col. He chuckled. 'You talked to Jo, and I talked to Col. What a couple of fools they must think us. Look at the pair of us. You'd think by our age we'd be able to get it right.'

'Wouldn't you? They say there's no fool like an old fool. I guess that goes for two old fools, too.'

'So,' he said, daringly, 'it was all right? I didn't offend you?'

'No, my dear.' There was a note George didn't recognise in Magda's voice, one he didn't recall ever hearing before, not in all the years he'd known her. 'I was worried you'd think…' it was Magda's turn to gaze intensely at the table, '…you'd think it was me, that I'd instigated it, that I had…' She looked up again.

George smiled tenderly. It was unusual for Magda to be lost for words, and this was the second time this morning. This new version of Magda was going to take some getting used to. But he was looking forward to the challenge.

Nineteen

Magda couldn't believe how relieved she felt. It was as if a gust of fresh air had suddenly blown away the cobwebs; the worries of the past few days disappeared, leaving in their place a sense of euphoria. If she closed her eyes, she could feel George's lips on hers again, the memory she'd tried so hard to dismiss. She looked across the table at his familiar face, at the lips she realised she'd never really seen properly before. She'd always known George was good looking, but he had been so much a part of her life – hers and Bill's – that she'd never looked at him properly.

Now she did, seeing the face, craggy with years, but still the handsome young man who had been her husband's best friend. As her eyes travelled down, from the eyes which held a tender expression, to his mouth, to the lips which had felt so soft, so right, on hers, she felt an unfamiliar shift somewhere inside. She wanted... she wanted him to kiss her again.

As if reading her mind, George said, 'Why don't we get out of here? Maybe go for a drive?'

Magda nodded, taking the opportunity to go to the ladies, while George paid both bills. Once there, she gazed at herself in the mirror expecting to see some sign of what had just happened. But the face looking back at her was the same as usual. Apart from a slight flush in her cheeks, there was no evidence her world had just shifted on its axis.

'We'll take the Prius,' George said, when she returned. 'It's more comfortable.'

Leaving Magda's ute outside the bakery, the pair walked to George's house to pick up his car. As they made their way along the familiar streets, George took Magda's hand in his, giving it a squeeze, which sent quivers of anticipation through her. How could his touch suddenly produce feelings that had lain dormant in her for years – feelings she'd never expected to experience again?

It wasn't as if they'd never touched before. But this touch was different. Things had changed between them. After their kiss and the admission of how they both felt, there could be no going back. Magda felt a tiny bubble of happiness simmer inside her, threatening to boil over into a full-blown explosion of unadulterated joy.

'Where would you like to go?' They were headed out of town when George glanced towards Magda.

'Anywhere.' It was enough just to be with him. How could they have wasted all those years? Magda knew they hadn't been wasted, but it had taken time away from each other to make them both realise what they could have together.

'I know a spot.' George stared at the road ahead and began to hum.

Magda smiled, suddenly more comfortable. This was the George she knew.

After a short drive, George pulled up in the parking lot beside a lake. Apart from one other car, it was deserted, though Magda suspected it would become busy later in the day. He helped her out, and they sauntered across to the edge of the lake where there were several benches and a picnic table.

'Bill and I used to come here for picnics when the boys were little,' Magda said, a note of regret in her voice.

'I'm sorry. Maybe this wasn't a good idea. Does it…?'

'No, it's fine, George. I think he'd have been pleased. Bill loved you. He'd have been delighted about how you've helped us – helped me – over the years. And now…' She turned to look at him.

George chuckled. 'You're right, the old devil would probably want to know why it had taken us so long.' He slung an arm around Magda's shoulders and drew her towards him.

For only a moment, Magda hesitated before allowing herself to sink into his embrace. It was an odd feeling, to be in the arms of her old friend. But it felt like she had come home – home to a place she knew so well, but had never really known.

'Oh, George,' she murmured, when they drew apart. 'Who'd have guessed?'

'I think we may be the only ones who didn't.' George gave a wry smile. 'There have been rumours about us for years.'

'True.' Magda laid her head against his chest, his chin resting on her hair.

'We might be more comfortable sitting down.' George led her to one of the benches where he took her in his arms again.

They sat like that till the sound of a car engine disturbed them. Magda sat up and patted her dishevelled hair. She checked her watch. 'We should be getting back. I need to see to the animals.'

'You and your animals!' George said fondly. 'I've always come second to them. I can't expect you to change now. But let's go.'

Magda bit her lip as they walked to the car. Was George right? Would she always put her animals first? They'd been her main companions for so long, it was difficult to know how her life might change.

'I'm sorry you feel that way – about my animals. I have to be concerned about them. They can't look after themselves. They depend on me.' She thought of the struggle she'd gone through to persuade the former owners to permit her to rescue her horses. She loved them with a fierce love, born out of the sadness of knowing what their fate might have been if she hadn't been successful in saving them.

Caesar and Brutus were different. They were like children to her. She'd seen a programme on television about *Friends of the Hound*, an organisation dedicated to the welfare of greyhounds. It made her weep for the plight of those lovely animals, and she immediately contacted them. Initially, she intended to offer a donation, but on checking out their website, had fallen in love with the creatures. A trip to Murwillumbah to check them out, and Caesar and Brutus had found their new home.

'It's okay, Magda. I understand. I love your animals, too.' He gave her shoulder a squeeze. 'I'd never want to come between you and your beasts.'

She glanced at him to see if he was joking, but George appeared to be as calm as usual, his lined face beaming down at her, convincing her all was well.

By the time she returned to Halcyon, it was late afternoon, and Caesar and Brutus were eager for their walk. Although they'd been outside all the time she'd been gone and were able to run around to their heart's content, they were happier wandering along the lane with her.

'Come on, then,' she said, putting down her bag and drinking a glass of water before setting off again.

Pleased to be enjoying the freedom of the lane, the dogs ran ahead leaving Magda with her thoughts. It had been a shock to learn George harboured the same sort of feelings she did, and an unfamiliar warmth flooded her. She began to sing as she walked along. She and George had decided to take things slowly so, even though it was tempting to move their budding relationship to the next step, they'd content themselves with a few kisses and cuddles for the time being.

But she knew neither of them would be able to let it remain that way for long.

Twenty

George was filled with renewed energy as he waved goodbye to Magda, her bright blue ute disappearing into the distance. He walked home slowly, chewing over what had happened. While he felt some embarrassment to think Col and Jo Ford might have been discussing them, at heart he was grateful for their interference. But for them, he and Magda might have been tiptoeing around each other for years to come. They might never have got together at all.

Now he could say they were in a relationship. It felt odd. He hadn't felt this way in a long time, not since Rose. And it was talk of Rose that had flung them together – Rose and Guy. But George knew what he felt for Magda was different from any youthful infatuation. Wasn't there a quote about putting away childish things? He hadn't been a child when he and Rose were together, but he knew he was a different person today from the student who'd wanted to marry her. Perhaps they wouldn't have stayed together; perhaps *she* had changed too. Maybe it had all been for the best, or was meant to be – as Magda would no doubt say.

When he arrived home, there was another email from New Zealand waiting for him. He fixed himself a coffee before settling down to read it. It was a very newsy email – from Anita this time with details of their trip to Australia. In addition to visiting George in Granite Springs, they intended to take trips to Sydney and Queensland's Sunshine Coast, and they wanted George to join them.

George re-read the invitation, tears coming to his eyes. He was amazed and humbled, at just how easily they'd included him in their family. It was as if there had been an empty spot, just waiting for him to fill it. Of course it helped that both Guy and Anita's parents had passed away. He was the only one left of the older generation. But he was still moved they wanted to include him in their lives.

He was about to compose a reply when another email arrived, this time from Guy suggesting a Skype call that evening. He emailed back his agreement, reflecting as he did so how adept he had become with the technology he'd always shunned. Having a family who lived so far away made a difference.

*

George turned off his computer. It had been wonderful seeing not only Guy, but also young Oliver who had insisted on talking to his grandad. George felt his eyes mist each time Oliver said it. It was a name he'd never dreamt he'd be called. Guy and Anita called him George, that was what he expected. He knew he could never replace the man who'd been Dad to Guy for all of his life up till now. But to hear Oliver call him Grandad was music to his ears.

'You will come with us to Sydney and Queensland, Grandad, won't you?' the young man asked. 'It won't be the same without you. We'll need you to translate for us,' he joked.

How could George refuse? It wasn't till the call finished and he was enjoying a glass of malt whisky that he thought of Magda. How would she feel about him going off with Guy and the others after Christmas? George had never had to consider another person before, not like this.

He scratched his head, then took another sip of his drink, rolling the smooth liquid around in his mouth. He'd keep quiet about it for now, he decided. Time enough to tell Magda closer to their visit. By then, he'd have a better idea of her reaction and – he stifled his distaste for deception– she'd have less opportunity to object.

Twenty-one

Magda was enjoying an early morning mug of camomile tea on the veranda before the sun grew too hot, when she saw a cloud of dust coming along the lane. She smiled as she recognised George's Prius, put down her tea and rose to welcome him.

To her surprise, she felt an unexpected thud of desire at the sight of George stepping out of his car. Seeing his white hair awry, his fit, tanned body in the khaki shorts and short-sleeved white shirt, his long, muscled legs ending in a pair of Birkenstocks, it was as if she was seeing him for the first time.

Caesar and Brutus padded over to greet him, and he patted their heads as he made his way to the house. There, he hugged Magda as if they'd been apart for weeks instead of less than twenty-four hours. As she leant into his embrace, she wondered how so much could have changed in one short week.

'Well then, what's on the agenda today?' George asked, cradling his usual cup of black coffee.

They were standing at the edge of the veranda gazing out across the paddocks to where the horses were grazing peacefully.

'It's going to be hot later on, but there's some weeding that needs to be done in the vegie garden and the salt blocks for the horses need to be replaced. The summer's hard on the poor creatures, even with the shade of the pepper trees. I wonder…' She gave George a wary glance.

'What is it?'

'I've been meaning to build shelters for them, but it always seemed too much work, then with the fire…'

'I can help. There's no need to exhaust yourself doing a man's work.'

Magda glared at him and drew herself up to her full height which was still several inches short of George's. 'What do you mean *a man's work?*'

'Sorry, sorry!' George put a hand up defensively. 'Just a manner of speaking. I didn't mean you weren't capable of doing it yourself. I know how skilful you are around this place, but it's not a sign of weakness to accept there are some things a stronger person might be able to do faster.'

'Hmm.' Magda wasn't sure that was what he meant but decided to give him the benefit of the doubt. And she had been procrastinating on that task because she was worried she wouldn't be able to manage it by herself.

'What do we need?'

'In the shed.' Magda led him to the galvanised steel shed she'd had installed when the house was built. It was a much sturdier framework than the old one which had perished in the fire and held, along with horse feed and garden implements, a collection of wooden posts and sheets of corrugated iron rescued from the tip.

'Waste not, want not, eh?' George helped her pull out what they required.

By the time Magda's list of tasks was completed it was late afternoon, and both were exhausted.

'Want a shower?' Magda asked, seeing the creases on George's face reamed with dirt and his hands and feet in a similar state.

'Actually,' he said, with a gleam in his eye. 'I booked a table for us at The Riverside. If you want to freshen up here, I can shower and change back home. I booked for six-thirty.'

'You old devil! You know I love it there. Won't be long. Help yourself to a beer while you're waiting. And maybe you could see to these two?' She nodded to where Caesar and Brutus were circling their empty food bowls impatiently.

Leaving George, Magda headed to the shower. It had been a good day. She and George worked well together. She knew that already. George had been helping her out for years. But today had been different. Today there was the added delight of their new situation. Their newfound closeness heightened the pleasure in everything they did together.

As the water cascaded over her, Magda examined her body critically. Could George find this old bat attractive? She drew in her stomach and cupped her drooping breasts, before releasing them again and letting out the breath she'd been holding. There was nothing she could do about it, and perhaps she was worrying needlessly; perhaps George wasn't thinking of… what she was thinking of.

She told herself she was being foolish to be concerned about something that hadn't happened, might never happen. Towelling herself dry, she pulled on a favourite dress. It was in a deep shade of cerise and suited her mood perfectly.

*

After a lovely dinner, Magda and George started walking to George's home. When they reached the house, Magda suddenly realised her ute was back at Halcyon. They'd driven to town in George's Prius.

'I can drive you back, or…' George gazed at Magda, his heart in his eyes.

She knew what he meant, but was she ready for this? She remembered the warmth that had flooded her when he stepped out of his car, the long-forgotten sensation of yearning for the feel of another body close to hers. But then she remembered her critical examination of herself in the shower.

Sensing her hesitation, George pulled her into his arms again. 'We're not getting any younger, Magda. Who knows how many more years we'll have together?'

Her head nestled into his chest. Inhaling the scent of him – a mixture of soap, shaving lotion and the wine they'd been drinking – Magda was torn between longing to be closer and the fear she'd prove a disappointment. It was years since she'd made love, since anyone – let alone a man – had seen her naked body. What if he was repulsed by the wrinkles, the rolls of fat, the…?

George seemed to understand. 'We're neither of us spring chickens. But I want you, Magda. I may be out of practice, but I think I can please you. Let me try?'

It was the right thing for him to say. All at once, Magda's fears were forgotten. All she could think of was this man; the man she'd known for so long; the man who wanted her as much as she wanted him.

'Yes,' she said, her voice muffled. Then she raised her head for his kiss.

Twenty-two

George lay awake for a long time, watching Magda sleep. He could scarcely believe what had happened. After her initial hesitation, Magda proved to be as eager as he was. Her desire matched his. Neither were as agile as they'd been as youngsters but in a strange way, it made their coming together even more pleasurable. They quickly adapted to each other's aging bodies and discovered a passion neither had anticipated. George had never thought to experience such sensual pleasure ever again.

He dropped a kiss on Magda's forehead, feeling her body shift towards his. He closed his eyes.

Morning came before he knew it, awakened as usual by the loud cawing of birds outside his window. George turned to look at the face beside him on the pillow to check he hadn't dreamt the whole thing.

But Magda was still there, sleeping soundly, her hair forming a white halo around her beautiful face. As he watched, her eyes opened and after a startled expression, she appeared to remember where she was.

'I wasn't dreaming?' she asked with a smile.

'Not at all, my love.' George kissed her forehead, his lips moving down over her eyelids to her mouth where they paused. With the softness of Magda's lips against his, George inhaled her unique scent – a mixture of the herbal fragrances that always surrounded her. Their tongues met, and he was lost again in the thrill, in the sensation of their bodies melting together as one.

Sitting over breakfast, George still couldn't believe his luck. He'd made what he considered to be his pièce de resistance – scrambled eggs with dried tomato and goats' cheese served on sour dough toast – and Magda had praised it, seemingly surprised at his prowess in the kitchen.

'You've never cooked much for me before now,' she said, tucking into the meal. 'But if we're to do this again, you'll have to stock up on some decent teas.' She sent a smiling glance in his direction as she sipped his favourite Earl Grey.

'I will. But I've been cooking for myself for years. Did you think I survive on takeaway and pre-cooked dinners?'

'I wasn't sure.' She grinned, and the warmth he felt in his heart for this woman he'd known for a lifetime astounded him.

He wasn't sure why he'd never invited Magda for a meal in the past. But it had been easier to get together for a quick cuppa – and she'd never complained about his choice of tea till now. Did that mean she intended to make a habit of this? He hoped so. In days gone by, they'd eaten out at her place. Magda was a great cook, though her predilection for vegetarian meals sometimes made him wish she was more flexible.

'I'll drive you home after breakfast. I know you need to take care of your animals,' he said.

'Thanks, George. You're a good man.'

They continued to eat in silence, George wondering how he could bring up the news he was heading off with Guy after Christmas. He hadn't mentioned it yet, reasoning it wouldn't matter that much. But things had changed. And Magda might consider he was abandoning her just when she wanted all of her family together – and that included George. He looked at her, still surrounded by the glow of their love-making, a glow he was all too conscious of, and decided to say nothing.

*

Back at Magda's, they were greeted by two dogs eager to be released from the house. Once outside, they cavorted around, following Magda and George into the paddock where she checked on the horses to ensure they had enough water, and George helped with fixing a loosened connection at the water trough. It was something that often happened when the animals knocked the stand, sometimes breaking the pipe, wasting water and leaving them thirsty.

'Thanks, George,' she said, when they returned to the house and the dogs had been fed and watered. 'We'll make a farmer of you yet.' She chuckled.

George knew she was joking but it set him thinking. He'd meant it when he told Magda they weren't getting any younger. He wondered how much longer she'd be able to cope with the heavy manual work looking after this acreage. Given their new arrangement – could he call it that? – perhaps they could look at pooling their resources. If they lived together – either here or in town – they could share the load of everyday life, be there for each other. He tucked that idea into the back of his mind. It was too soon to broach it now – but soon.

On the way out from town, they'd stopped to buy the weekend papers. With the animals all happy, Magda brewed herself some tea and coffee for George. They settled in her new cane chairs on the veranda, the dogs at their feet. *Like an old married couple*, George thought.

'This is nice,' he said, after some time. 'It feels different, now we…'

'It is different. But…'

'But?' George's heart sank. Was she having doubts?

'It takes a bit of getting used to. You see…' she twirled a silver curl in her fingers, '…in my mind, you've always been Bill's friend – even after he was gone – Bill's friend, the boys' uncle. Now…' she glanced at him sideways, '…it's as if you belong to me. You're *my* friend, my…'

'Sweetheart? Lover?' His mouth felt dry.

'I guess so.' Magda smiled, and the dogs raised their heads as if knowing something important was being said.

George dropped his paper and moved to take Magda in his arms again. 'I think I need something stronger than coffee.'

'I don't have any of your malt whisky in the house,' she said. 'But perhaps some wine… or champagne. It is close to lunchtime, and I think we have something to celebrate. Why don't I fix a platter of bread and cheeses while you pop the cork on the bottle of *Yellow* that's been languishing in the fridge since I moved in?'

Champagne sounded good to George and perhaps, afterwards, he could tempt her back to bed, to *her* bed this time. After many years of celibacy, he was keen to discover if last night had been a one-off, or a sign of things to come.

Twenty-three

It was three weeks now since she and George had first spent the night together, and Magda was full of the joys of life. She'd already purchased all the non-perishable items for Christmas, along with gifts for the family, and George would be arriving soon to help her put up the Christmas tree. Then they planned to go together to the lighting of the town's tree beside the war memorial in the centre of town. When she'd been doing her shopping, the bare tree was already in place and the council workers were busily decorating the lampposts with poinsettia wreaths. It really felt as if Christmas was on its way.

'Anyone home?' Jo Ford's voice came through the open kitchen door. The dogs raised their heads before dropping them again to resume their naps.

Magda turned from where she'd been wrapping gifts for her grandchildren. The radio was blaring out Christmas carols and she hadn't heard the car. 'Jo!' Magda was flustered. She hadn't spoken to Jo since her massage when Jo had offered her advice. She'd been meaning to thank her but the opportunity hadn't arisen and, unusually for her, Magda had been too self-conscious to make the first move. 'Come in,' she said, unnecessarily. Jo was already in the kitchen.

'You've been a stranger these past few weeks. I thought I should drop by to make sure you were all right.'

'I'm fine – as you can see.' While Magda was grateful she had neighbours who were concerned about her welfare, it did irk her to be considered in the *at risk* category of elderly people who needed to be checked on. 'I've been busy preparing for Christmas. But it's time for me to take a break. Would you like a cuppa?'

'That would be lovely. I'm about to brave the shops myself and a cup of your divine herbal tea would put me in the right mind to deal with the Christmas rush. I know it's only the beginning of December, but preparations seem to get earlier every year. You're still expecting the family?'

Magda nodded.

'Well,' Jo said, when they were seated on the veranda with cups of peppermint tea and a tempting plate of recently baked fruit loaf, 'did you talk – you and George?'

'We did.' Magda clasped her cup in both hands.

'And?' The question should have sounded prying, but, coming from Jo, it didn't.

But that didn't mean Magda was about to reveal her innermost feelings. Some things were best kept private. 'We sorted things out,' she said.

'Good.' Jo glanced at Magda, but seeing her buttoned-up lips, clearly decided not to pursue it. 'I see you have your tree,' she said, referring to the two-metre tree leaning against the side of the house.

'Yes,' Magda beamed. 'It was delivered this morning. Maybe a tad early, but I love the scent of pine in the house.'

'Would you like Col to pop over to help? It looks pretty big.'

'It's bigger than I am, you mean?' Magda chortled. 'Thanks, Jo. But George is coming out to help put it up. In fact…' she rose, cup in hand, and looked towards the gate where a white car was driving through, '…that's him, now.'

'Well, maybe I should go.' Jo finished her tea and rose too. 'We'll see you at the tree lighting tonight, I expect?'

'Wouldn't miss it.' Magda gave Jo a hug, just as George's car pulled up. 'And thanks for your advice,' she whispered with a smile.

'Jo!' George greeted her as she stepped into her car. 'I hope I'm not driving you away.'

'Not at all, George. I was just leaving. I need to get into town.'

But Magda saw Jo give her a complicit glance. She winced.

'What's the matter, love?' George pulled Magda into a hug as Jo drove off. 'Not annoying you, was she? Not like Jo.'

'No, nothing like that.' Magda brushed away her concern. Everyone was going to find out about them soon, anyway – find out the rumours were true after all. She didn't care – or did she? Despite what others might think, Magda was a very private person. She hated the idea of her love life being bandied around by the town gossips. But it was bound to happen once she and George were seen everywhere together. The tree lighting tonight would be just the beginning.

'This it, then?' George gestured to the tree. 'Let's get it inside.'

But manoeuvring the tree inside and setting it into place wasn't as easy as they'd anticipated, hampered as they were by the two dogs who seemed to think this was a new game.

Finally, it was done. The tree stood proudly in the corner of the living room, and Magda and George stood back to admire their efforts, George's arm around Magda's shoulders.

'Do you want to start decorating it?' George asked. 'I can help. I don't want you climbing up to reach those high branches. What if you fell?'

'What if *you* fell?' Magda asked, and they both laughed. 'No, I'll do it later, there's no rush. I bought some new decorations. The old ones…' She fell silent remembering the treasured items, collected over a lifetime, which had perished in the fire. Then she mentally gave herself a shake. 'What about some lunch?'

'Sounds good, but first…' George pulled Magda close and gave her a kiss. 'That's better,' he said with a grin. 'It feels so natural to hold and kiss you like this. I'm not sure why it took us so long.'

'Timing. The time wasn't right till now.' Magda slipped out of his arms and went through to the kitchen, George and the two dogs following. She shooed Caesar and Brutus out the door and closed the screen door behind them. 'That'll keep them out of our way for a bit. They've had enough excitement for today.'

*

At five minutes to six, Magda and George joined the crowds by the war memorial in the middle of Main Street to watch the lighting of the town Christmas tree. It had been a hot day and was beginning to cloud over with the threat of rain, but that hadn't deterred the people of Granite Springs from gathering to participate in the annual event which signified the beginning of a month of festivities.

The lighting of the tree itself would be followed by music performed by some of Owen Larsen's students from the university. Then in subsequent weeks, there would be the student performance of Cinderella, a special race meeting, a family picnic to be held by the riverbank in conjunction with a race down the river of craft made entirely from spare tyres, and culminating with the performance of the Messiah the weekend before Christmas. The community of Granite Springs knew how to celebrate.

Magda and George found themselves jostled by the friendly crowds as they sought vantage spots. She was glad of George's strong hands around her waist as he pulled her back against him, protecting her from the crush of bodies. But she did see a few people glancing knowingly their way and a few raised eyebrows. She merely shrugged and leant more closely against George, grateful for his broad chest and firm grasp.

At six o'clock precisely, there was the combined 'Oooh' of hundreds of voices as the tree suddenly exploded in a burst of brightly coloured lights. Immediately, the band of students began playing a selection of Christmas carols, followed by the spirited rendition of some old favourites. The crowd gradually drifted away leaving a few stalwarts, Magda and George, Jo and Col among them. When the music changed to the sound of *The Way You Look Tonight*, George opened his arms, and Magda allowed herself to be led into the square where several couples were already dancing.

As George hummed the melody, then softly sung the words into her ear, Magda felt like she was seventeen again. The years fell away. The other dancers disappeared. It was as if they were alone in the world. Her body was flooded with warmth and an almost forgotten sweet pleasure. She wished it would never stop.

'Look at you two!'

Col's voice in her ear made Magda realise the music had stopped, and so had George. But they were still in each other's arms.

'No need to ask if you're a couple,' Col said, while Jo tried to shush him.

Magda blushed, but George only grinned.

'I know,' he said. 'You're thinking it took us long enough.' He kept hold of Magda. 'But this little lady was worth waiting for.'

'We're going to have dinner at The Riverside. Join us?' Jo asked, smiling gently. 'Tonight is a cause for celebration.'

Magda wasn't sure to what she was referring – the tree lighting or George and her being seen together like this in public. She decided it didn't matter and looked to George for guidance. They had talked about having dinner after the tree lighting but had made no definite plans.

'I'm game,' he said. 'Magda?'

'Sounds lovely, Jo.' Magda disentangled herself from George and patted her hair. Then she glanced around to see who'd been watching. To her relief, there were no eyes on them, everyone else too busy with their own friends and family to bother with what she and George had been doing. She smiled at the man who was positively glowing. *It's going to be a wonderful Christmas*, she thought.

Twenty-four

George knew he had to tell Magda about his proposed trip with Guy and family. It had been a few weeks now, and they were getting on so well he didn't want to spoil it. But she had to know. Perhaps she wouldn't mind too much. After all, her own family would be here in Granite Springs. She'd never cared before if their plans hadn't matched up. But they hadn't been sleeping together before, he reminded himself.

George remembered how Magda's body felt against his, how they'd discovered a passion beyond his imaginings, how... He wondered what Bill would think about them getting together. Well, Bill couldn't say they'd rushed into it. It had been years, decades, since Bill's death. George had taken his time before he'd made a move on his old friend's widow. But he was glad he had; glad they'd found a way to be together.

But it wasn't enough. George wanted to seal the deal, make a more permanent arrangement. He was too old for this shilly-shallying, spending some nights here and some out at Halcyon so Magda could take care of her animals. He wanted to stay in one place, whichever one that might be. He wanted to spend every night with her – every day too.

George made up his mind. He'd talk to her tonight, make the suggestion, propose they lived together – propose marriage, because that was what he wanted. But, first, he needed to tell her about the trip.

*

After another evening of lovemaking in George's bed, followed by a night sleeping in each other's arms, George felt it safe to broach the subject of his proposed trip north. Magda's reaction surprised him.

'You're going to do what?' Her voice rose in an anguished howl. 'But… It's Christmas the boys will be here. I thought…'

'We won't be leaving till after Christmas.' George attempted to temper the shock. 'Anita has arranged for us to fly up to Sydney at the end of December. We'll bring in the new year there, see the fireworks. It's something I've always fancied doing. Then a week on the Sunshine Coast on the beach at Noosa. I'll be back before you know I've been gone. You'll be busy with *your* family while I spend time with mine.' George held his breath waiting for Magda's reply. He still couldn't say the words *my family* without a thrill of pride.

'But…' Magda rolled away from him, clearly upset.

George sighed. He'd been aware of Magda's lack of enthusiasm for the appearance of Guy and Oliver in his life. Initially, he'd put it down to her surprise, but as time went on and she still seemed reluctant to share his excitement, he'd tried to pretend he was imagining it. Now, he knew he needed to do something, say something, to make her know how important she was to him. He took a deep breath.

'Magda, sweetheart, I've been thinking.'

She didn't move, but George could tell she was listening. He pulled her around and took her face in his hands. He kissed her forehead, his lips travelling down to meet hers, which she stubbornly kept tightly closed.

'Sweetheart. I don't want to be away from you. You do know that, I hope. But… I couldn't refuse… Anita had already made the booking. You do understand, don't you?' He felt Magda weaken, a release of the tension in her body and decided to press his advantage. 'I love you. I want to be with you – always – to spend every day with you. I want to…' He took a deep breath. 'Will you marry me?'

There was no reply. George held his breath. Had he been too hasty? Was it too soon? Had he misjudged Magda's feelings for him?

'Oh, George,' she said at last, pulling away from him and sitting up. 'I love you, too. But why do things need to change? Why can't we leave things as they are? There's no need to change everything, is there?'

George gazed at the woman he loved more than life itself. Her stubbornness was one of the things he loved about her. But he was getting worn out travelling back and forwards, never knowing where he'd be spending the night. He wanted to stay in one place, to know it was home, and to know Magda was in it. He saw her lips – the lips he loved to kiss – form a slight pout.

'Are you unhappy with things the way they are?' she asked.

'I love being with you. Is it wrong to want to be with you all the time?'

'I'm not sure, George. I've lived on my own for so long, I've become accustomed to doing everything my way. I don't think I'd be much good at sharing. I think I've become too set in my ways, too independent to allow...' She bit her lip.

'Will you at least think about it?'

A crease appeared between Magda's eyes, tempting George to stroke it away, to take back his proposal. But he couldn't do that. It was too important to him. If Magda didn't want them to live together, could he continue as they were? He saw the years stretch out ahead of them – years during which they became older and frailer – perhaps unable to make the trips to see each other. It didn't bear thinking about. He conveniently forgot that's how life would be if they hadn't shared their feelings for each other, had never begun their loving relationship, had remained merely good friends.

'I can't think about it now.' Magda swung her legs out of bed, and George watched as she pulled on the garments she'd cast aside so readily the previous evening. 'I have to get home and...' she faced him, her mouth set in the stubborn line he knew so well, '...I want to be on my own today – for a few days. I'll see you at the performance on Saturday. I'll call you before then.'

George watched her go, heard the door slam and the engine of her blue ute start. He flopped back on the pillows with a sigh. Why had he opened his mouth? If he'd kept quiet – about his trip and his desire for them to be married, they'd probably have made love again this morning. Magda would still be in his arms; he'd be whispering sweet nothings into her ear.

But their future would still not be resolved.

Twenty-five

Damn George! Magda drove off with more speed than she intended, startling a couple of galahs who'd chosen to pick at some seeds in the middle of the road. Why did he want to change things – just as life was so good?

It had been a big step to allow a man into her life again after so many years. But it was George, a man she thought she knew almost as well as she knew herself. Obviously not! She stamped on the brake as the only traffic light on Main Street turned red, forcing her to pay attention to the road.

She'd believed George was as happy with their arrangement as she was. It worked perfectly. Over the past few weeks, she and George had settled into a routine whereby they'd spend a couple of weeknights at his house in town and the weekend out at Halcyon where he helped Magda with her animals and vegetable garden and joined her and the dogs in their walks. It was a shock to discover he wanted it to change.

Then there was this business with his trip. Well, she wasn't going to let that worry her. But it did. Magda couldn't stifle the resentment she felt every time George mentioned *his* family. It was as if he was rubbing in the fact he now had a family, he didn't need Magda's family any longer. In her heart, she knew it wasn't true. His feelings towards her sons hadn't changed – or his feelings towards her. His proposal of marriage proved that. But still… it rankled he'd been so quick to make plans without consulting her.

A flicker of anger built up inside her as she drove along the road towards Halcyon, blind today to the beauty of the bales of hay stacked in the paddocks and the colourful flowers growing wild by the roadside. Magda wasn't sure whether she was angry with George or herself. How could she – the woman who'd built a reputation for giving advice to others – be so clueless about her own life as not to have foreseen how George would react to discovering he had fathered a son, and to their budding relationship? Characteristics of George she'd always admired were his appreciation of the importance of family, his loyalty, his innate sense of decency and his strong moral compass. She should have realised he wouldn't be content to continue the casual relationship they'd formed.

Magda had calmed down somewhat by the time she drove through her own gate. She was glad to reach the house and let Caesar and Brutus out. She tried to put George out of her mind as she filled their food and water bowls, then headed for the shower.

It was when the dogs were happily fed and watered and lying out in the sun, and she was enjoying her second cup of calming camomile tea that she received a call from Adelaide.

'Mum.'

It was good to hear Kenny's voice, almost as if he'd known she needed reassurance from one of her own family. But there was something in Kenny's tone that disturbed her.

'Is everything all right?' she asked, her imagination going into overdrive, before settling down again. What could be wrong? Kenny and Laura were planning to travel up with the boys in a week's time, arriving on Christmas Eve. Everything was prepared. They were to stay with her, and she had booked rooms in town for Scott's family, although she expected they'd spend most of their time at Halcyon.

'I'm sorry, Mum.' Kenny sighed.

Magda could picture her son, no doubt sitting in his office, trying to work out how to give his mother the bad news without hurting her. He was a good boy at heart, but often had trouble with being tactful.

'It's about Christmas…'

Magda's heart dropped.

'We can't come. I know you were counting on us, that you wanted us all together this year, but Laura's mum's taken ill. The nursing home contacted us. We need to be here for her. I know you're all prepared but I'm sure you'll understand.'

Magda gazed out the window at the new shoots peeking through in the vegetable garden, the horses grazing in the paddock. She took a deep breath before replying. 'I'm sorry about Laura's mum,' she said, trying to stifle her disappointment.

'You can come to us again instead.'

Magda winced, remembering the previous year, glad she had a good reason to refuse. 'No honey, that's not possible, Scott will be here with Tara, Chloe and Holly.'

'You haven't heard?'

'Heard what?' Magda's heart sank yet again.

'He said he'd let you know. They've all come down with food poisoning.'

Magda felt herself begin to crumble. Scott wasn't coming either?

She ended the call in a daze. For several minutes, she sat staring into space, till her two dogs, sensing something was wrong, pushed their noses into her lap.

'Oh, you dears,' she said, tears pricking at her eyes. 'Looks like it'll be just us for Christmas this year. What am I going to do with all the food?'

Then her usual optimism took over and she rose. She hadn't checked her emails since she got back. No doubt Scott had sent her one while she'd been at George's place.

George! She knew he'd be happy to include her in his Christmas celebration, but she didn't think she could stand it. It would be almost as bad as being in Adelaide – to be the odd one out in George's new family. No, she wouldn't tell him. She'd let him think they were all coming as planned, let him find out afterwards. She'd work out what to say then.

Banishing the dogs outside, Magda headed to her studio where she fired up the computer. Sure enough, there was a long email from Scott full of apologies.

We're so disappointed, Mum. It was a seafood meal we had for Tara's birthday. Only Holly missed out as she was still in university. But there's no way we'll be well enough to make the trip. Tara has been particularly sick, and little Chloe…

Magda read on, feeling sympathy for her Canadian family. Christmas wasn't going to be much fun for them. When she finished, she expelled the breath she'd been holding. She needed to put this behind her and get on with life. She had two clients coming for their massage this afternoon. They'd expect her to be her usual positive and optimistic self. She lit her bergamot and lavender candles, closed her eyes and breathed in their familiar scents allowing their gentle fragrances to soothe her, just as they soothed her clients.

When she opened her eyes again, she had the strangest, yet very strong feeling that all this was happening for a reason. She swallowed her disappointment, knowing how fate often worked in mysterious ways, even though she couldn't imagine what good could come from her plans for Christmas being disrupted.

*

As usual, Magda felt much better once her clients had left, both assuring her how much she'd helped them. It was a good feeling, helping people in her new home, to be appreciated for her efforts. And, she told herself, she had no need to share that with anyone. What George suggested was an unnecessary complication in their life. Surely, once he had time to consider, he'd come to the same conclusion. Then they could just continue as before.

'Come, Caesar, Brutus,' she called, walking outside. The two dogs came bounding to greet her from where they'd been lying in a shady spot on the veranda. A brisk walk would help her prepare for the call she knew she must make. It had been unfair of her to leave George in such a temper, but she knew if she hadn't, she might have said something she'd regret. Now she'd had time to reflect, and could hopefully convince him to come around to her way of thinking.

The trio had almost reached the gate to Yarran when they met Jo and her dog, Scout, coming from the other direction. Glad to see each other, the dogs began to sniff around their friends while Magda and Jo stopped to chat.

'Why don't you come in for a cuppa?' Jo asked after a few minutes. 'The dogs are happy to be together. It's good for Scout to have company once and a while. I'm sure he gets lonely with just Col and me.'

Magda wasn't so sure, but recognised Jo's desire to talk, so agreed.

Once they were seated in Jo's family kitchen with cups of Jo's favourite Earl Grey tea, Magda found herself unburdening to Jo yet again. What was it about the woman that invited confidences?

'So you see how selfish I am,' she finished. 'I resent George spending time with the family he's just met and, when he wants us to live together – to get married – I treat him as if he's made an indecent suggestion. But…' she raised her eyes to meet Jo's, '…I'm so set in my ways, Jo. How could I possibly change – give up my independence – even for George? How did you do it – for Col?'

She waited while Jo took a sip of tea then carefully placed her cup down again on the scrubbed pine table. 'I think it may have been different for me, Magda,' she said carefully. 'Like you and George, Col and I had known each other most of our lives. But I hadn't been on my own as long as you have. Gordon and I had only been separated for five years when Col and I got together. I do know what you mean about being set in your ways, however. Even in those few years I'd made a life for myself, a life which didn't need a man in it, I'd become quite self-sufficient before Col arrived on the scene.'

Magda remembered. She remembered how she'd had a premonition Jo and Col would get together before it happened, and how she'd been happy for Jo, felt it was so right.

Jo remembered too. 'You told me you'd do the same if you were my age and had a man like Col interested in you,' she reminded her.

Magda's words had come back to haunt her. 'Ah, but I'm not your age. I can give you at least ten years. And I think George and I are fine the way we are. I don't know that I want a man cluttering up my life and my house – no matter how attractive he is.'

'And George is a good-looking man.' Jo grinned.

'I can't argue with that. He's a good man too. But I really can't see myself changing my life around for him.'

'Well, we're all different. But I've never regretted marrying Col and I don't think it would have mattered what age we were or how independent I felt. I do hope you and George manage to sort things out. It's sad to be alone when you get old.'

Col appeared at that point, and the conversation turned to his herd of alpacas and how delighted he was with them, planning to take a couple to next year's Granite Springs Show as a special attraction.

'They are such gentle creatures,' he said, 'and the children will love to lead them around and feed them. Jo's grandkids love them to bits.'

'We'll see you at the Messiah on Saturday?' Jo asked, when Magda finally rose to leave, reminding her of her vow to call George.

She knew he was worried about the performance. Even though he was no longer the conductor of the Granite Springs Choristers, he still felt a degree of ownership, and Owen had been good about involving him in the preparations for this special event. 'Of course. George would never forgive me if I missed it. And I do love the atmosphere in the church at this time of year – and the music. It's so special.'

As she walked back along the lane, the dogs at her heel, Magda thought Jo was right about one thing. Everyone was different. And while Jo was happy to give up her independence for marriage with Col, it wasn't for Magda. She just hoped she could make George see reason.

Opening her own gate, Magda also realised she hadn't told Jo her family would no longer be here for Christmas. If she had, no doubt Jo would have invited her to join them for the day. Magda would have hated that, too. She didn't want anyone's charity.

Twenty-six

George hung up the phone with a wry grin. While he was pleased Magda had called, he still didn't understand her reluctance to make their relationship more permanent. Okay, she might not want marriage; perhaps they were a bit long in the tooth – though he rather liked the idea. But surely there was nothing to stop them living together? He could see why she might not want to move into town, but he'd made it clear he was willing to live at Halcyon.

He scratched his head. He didn't pretend to understand women, how their minds worked. And he certainly didn't understand Magda. After all those years of friendship, he thought he had her worked out, but she'd surprised him with her refusal to reconsider her decision. He'd go along with it, of course he would. He couldn't imagine what his life would be like without Magda in it. He'd missed her so much during the past year, been afraid she'd decide to stay in Adelaide – or even move to Canada to be with Scott.

It had been a relief to get the email telling of her return. And now they'd moved on. Moved on to a relationship he'd only dreamed about. He knew he should be happy for what they had, but he wouldn't be human if he didn't yearn for more.

But he had other things to think about. It was only two days till the Messiah, then Guy and his family would be arriving the following week. He was disappointed they wouldn't be here for the performance, but was looking forward to meeting Anita and Oliver in the flesh and to introducing them all to Magda. He was sure she'd change her strangely distant attitude once she actually met them. He planned to take them out to Halcyon on Boxing Day, then they could meet Magda's family. He seemed to recall there had been some talk of getting together with Jo's family too. A big family gathering was exactly what they all needed, in the true spirit of Christmas. He couldn't wait.

*

All too soon, Saturday arrived. George awoke in Magda's bed and, for a few moments, forgot her stubbornness of the past few days as he curled up behind her, his arms around her waist, his lips on her skin as he inhaled her familiar sweet fragrance. She turned towards him and their lips met. Why had he been so worried? Why wasn't this enough? There was still a niggle in the back of his mind making him wonder why Magda was so resistant to making this permanent.

It was a pity they couldn't stay here all day. They both had things to take care of. Magda had her animals, and he'd promised to call in on Owen after breakfast. Despite his customary laidback attitude, the younger man was nervous about tonight's performance, and George had promised to go over the final details with him before he went back to town.

After a delicious breakfast of a mushroom and basil omelette with grilled tomatoes and a slice of Magda's home-baked bread, washed down with coffee, George felt ready to face the day, despite what he took to be a slight feeling of heartburn. 'You're making my heart ache,' he joked as he kissed Magda goodbye. 'See you this evening.' He gave her another hug. Perhaps she'd change her mind after Christmas.

'Wouldn't miss it.'

George drove off. He could have walked to Owen's, but knew Magda was planning to be busy for the rest of the day and he intended to spend it buying gifts for Guy, Anita and Oliver, something he'd been procrastinating about, unsure what they'd like. Magda's suggestion of books about Australia was a good one, and the photo book he'd ordered had arrived, but he wanted something more personal too. He also needed to buy food supplies.

'Hey, George!' Owen sauntered out to greet him. 'Good to see you. There are a few things…'

Almost two hours passed before Fran popped her head around the door. 'Are you two still at it? How about some lunch?'

'Sounds good. George?' Owen asked.

George didn't feel hungry. Maybe it was the big breakfast he'd eaten, or perhaps he was being influenced by Owen's anxiety. 'Not for me. I should be getting back. I have a few things to take care of before tonight. It's all going to be fine, Owen. It's natural to be worried but you've no need.'

'Thanks.' Owen slapped him on the shoulder.

'Thanks, George,' Fran said. 'I've never seen Owen like this. He's usually full of confidence. It'll be great, honey,' she said, putting her arm around Owen's waist. Their obvious happiness made George more determined than ever to change Magda's mind. It was crazy for them to be flitting between houses like teenagers, when there was no reason for them not to be together – apart from Magda's fear of losing her independence. In his view, independence was overrated. He'd settle for companionship any day.

*

George still wasn't feeling great. What he'd put down to heartburn after breakfast at Magda's had been bothering him on and off all day. The tablets he'd taken seemed to have had no effect. Maybe it wasn't heartburn at all. But he couldn't afford to be ill at this time of year, not with Guy arriving in a few days' time. Maybe he'd check in with his doctor just to be on the safe side.

The church was almost full and was buzzing with the sound of excited voices when George arrived. He stopped in the doorway, his eyes roaming around, taking in the large Christmas tree in one corner, the nativity scene in another, and the choristers filing into place. They looked superb, the women in their black skirts, the men in black trousers, and all wearing red tops of one sort or another. George's heart swelled with pride. He might no longer be their conductor, but this was the choir he'd formed and nurtured.

'George.' He felt Magda slip her hand into his, and turned to her with a smile. Her returned smile told him she understood exactly what he was feeling. He gave her hand a squeeze.

They walked up the aisle together to the seats Owen had reserved for them in the front pew and settled down to enjoy the performance.

It all went beautifully, and George felt his heart soar as what he still considered to be *his* choristers rose to the occasion, their voices blending perfectly in the rousing harmonic chorus. As the evening neared its end, George became conscious of a sense of weariness then, as the choir took their final bow and he rose along with the rest of the audience, a paralysing pain gripped his chest, radiating to his left shoulder and arm.

He put out a hand towards Magda and was aware of her turning towards him, her eyes filled with concern…

Twenty-seven

'George!'

George suddenly clasped his chest and collapsed back into the pew just as the choir were receiving their well-deserved accolade from the audience. Magda looked around wildly, catching the eye of her local doctor who immediately recognised what was happening, and hurried over.

'Heart attack,' he muttered, taking one look at George as he lay back on the wooden seat. 'We need to get him to hospital.'

Magda felt as if time slowed down. She was vaguely aware of voices, of George being carried off on a stretcher while the church fell silent out of respect. She wanted to yell, *He isn't dead! He can't be dead!* but swallowed the words. What if he was? How could she survive without her best friend?

The next few hours were a blur.

'Are you all right?'

Magda heard Jo's voice as if it was coming from a long distance away. She shook her head to try to clear the cotton wool which seemed to be filling it. 'Is he…?' she managed to say, dreading the answer.

'George is going to be fine. The doctor said it was a mild attack. It was lucky it happened where it did. Though it'll be one Messiah we won't forget in a hurry.'

'Can I see him?' Magda gazed around the dimly lit corridor where she was seated along with Jo, Col, Owen and Fran. She had no recollection of getting here, or of how the cardboard cup of cooling tea got into her hand.

'He's in surgery,' Col said. 'An angioplasty, the doctor said. I think that involves putting in a stent.' His voice was patient as if repeating something she should already know.

Magda had a vague recollection of having heard this before. What was happening to her? Was she losing her mind? It was George who was ill, not her.

'Your tea is cold. Let me get you a fresh cup.' Jo took the cup from her.

Magda shook her head. What she craved was a cup of her own camomile or peppermint tea to calm and restore her, not this sad excuse for tea from a vending machine. She knew she'd never see a cardboard cup again without remembering this night.

'You don't all need to be here,' she said. 'I'll stay until I know how George is. I'll be fine,' she added as Jo tried to object.

They all stayed for a bit longer, then Owen and Fran left. Jo and Col insisted Magda shouldn't be alone and despite protesting, she was glad of their company.

After what seemed like forever, a doctor appeared to tell them George was in recovery. 'He'll sleep when he gets back to the ward. It's best you all go home and come back in the morning,' he said, no doubt accustomed to dealing with anxious relatives.

But they weren't relatives, only friends. For the first time, Magda saw that there might be wisdom in George's suggestion, the one she'd dismissed so easily. A heart attack was serious. George's had been minor. But what if it had been more serious, if he was gravely ill and only relatives were allowed to see him? How could she have borne it?

Reluctantly, they left the hospital, only to stop in the car park. Magda looked around for her ute, before remembering she hadn't driven there. She'd come with Jo and Col. Her ute was still at the church.

'Let us drive you home,' Jo said. 'I don't think you should be behind the wheel. You're still in shock.'

Trembling with a combination of shock and exhaustion, Magda allowed Jo to help her into their car and drive her back home.

Caesar and Brutus were asleep when Magda opened the door after waving Col and Jo off. They raised their heads at the sound of her coming in, then sensing her distress rose to push their noses into her hands. 'Oh, you dear things. What would I do without you?' But her thoughts were with George not her dogs, as she patted them both then made herself a cup of camomile tea, taking it through to the bedroom.

She doubted she'd get much sleep in what was left of the night. There were decisions to be made, decisions which would change the habits of a lifetime. It had taken the thought of losing George to make Magda realise how selfish she had been. John Donne had been right. *No man was an island.* She now knew she and George needed each other. It had occurred to her at the hospital it could just as easily have been *her* lying there.

If she had been in George's place, Magda knew he wouldn't have hesitated to move heaven and earth to make things right for her. He'd have moved in to take care of her, and that's what she must do for him. She couldn't leave her animals, so he must come here. And his family must come for Christmas, too.

How lucky she had enough room for them all. Magda remembered what crossed her mind when her own family cancelled their travel plans – everything happened for a reason. She shivered as she realised that, if her own Christmas plans hadn't fallen apart, she wouldn't have been able to take in George and his family.

Surprisingly, Magda did manage to get a few hours' sleep, whether due to the calming effect of the tea or the decision she'd made. How foolish she'd been to imagine her independence meant more to her than her old friend.

Magda was up early and, deciding not to wait for Jo and Col, she called a taxi. By the time she'd let the dogs have a run and made sure they had enough food and water for the day, she heard her ride arrive. Taking a deep breath, she headed out.

The ride into town was fraught with worry. Perhaps she should have called the hospital first. But what good would it have done? Magda had no intention of sitting patiently at home waiting for news. This was George, the man she loved, the man she now knew she wanted to be with forever, even if it meant giving up her independence. She had no idea what the prognosis might be, if her friend and companion would be left weaker, would need permanent care. Whatever the future held, she vowed she'd be there for him. They'd be there for each other. George's collapse had suddenly made Magda aware of her own mortality.

Twenty-eight

George opened his eyes to discover he was lying in a hospital bed hooked up to a number of machines which bleeped and hissed. He tried to remember what happened, but his last memory was of being at the performance of the Messiah, standing up to applaud, then feeling this agonising pain.

A nurse appeared in the doorway. 'You're awake, George. How are you feeling this morning?'

'Tired. Have I…? Am I…?'

'You suffered a minor heart attack last night. Fortunately, you were brought in immediately and the surgeon performed an emergency angioplasty and inserted a stent. You'll feel tired for a few days, but we'll have you home for Christmas.' She gave him a grin and wheeled over a trolley to check his vital signs.

Christmas! It was almost Christmas. Guy would be arriving in two days' time and he was stuck here in hospital.

'When…?' He tried to sit up.

'Now, don't try to move too quickly. Mr Wallace, the consultant who performed your surgery, will be coming to see you tomorrow. He'll decide when you can be discharged.'

'But…' George fell back against the pillows. He certainly didn't feel like going anywhere. But what was he going to do?

After the nurse left, he lay contemplating how fate had a way of bringing you down to earth. He'd been on cloud nine since meeting his son, his exhilaration only dimmed by Magda's attitude, one he was sure he could change. Then this happened.

As the image of Magda filled his thoughts, the real Magda walked into the room, her face drawn with concern.

'George!' She hurried to his bedside. 'You gave us such a fright. It's so good to see you…'

'Alive?' he asked, with a weak smile. 'It's not so easy to get rid of me.'

Magda leant over to kiss him on the forehead, her lips soft and warm on his skin. 'I'm sorry,' she said. 'I was wrong… to be so resistant to your suggestion… your proposal. I'm still not sure about marriage. We may be too old for all that malarkey – and you'd have to move out to Halcyon, but…' She smiled, a smile that lit up her face.

Trust Magda. Even now, when he was lying in bed, recovering from a heart attack, she managed to be laying down the rules. But he didn't care. He was so happy to see her, to hear she'd changed her mind.

'Anything you say, dear.' He grinned and took her hand in his. 'But I'm not going to be up to much for some time. Christmas…'

'Don't worry about anything. You can come straight to Halcyon when they let you out of this place.' Her eyes roamed around the clinical room with distaste. 'And your New Zealand family can come there, too. We can all have Christmas at Halcyon.'

'But…' George hadn't forgotten Magda's family, '…you'll have Scott and Kenny and…'

Magda touched a finger to his lips. 'They're not coming. I didn't want to tell you, to admit they'd let me down. Oh, they have good enough reasons, illness etcetera, but…' She bit her lip. 'Well, enough about that. It means I have plenty of room for you and your lot.'

'I can't let you do that.'

'I don't see how you can stop me.' She chuckled, her old familiar chuckle. 'You're stuck in here, and I bet the consultant will say you need someone to take care of you when you go home. You can't go back to an empty house and you can't expect Guy and his family to look after you.'

Magda was right – as usual. The only time she hadn't been was when she refused to live with him. Now it seemed she'd even seen the light about that. All because of this heart attack. Maybe it hadn't been such a bad thing after all. But he'd rather he hadn't had to go through it for Magda to see the light.

'We'll see.'

Magda remained at his bedside till a hospital employee arrived with his lunch and he discovered he was hungry.

'Look at the time.' Magda rose. 'I expect you think I've been here long enough. I can come back later, and you can fill me in on when you'll be out and when Guy is due to arrive. Is there anything I can get you?'

'Maybe the book I was reading – it's by my bed. My keys…' He looked around, but Magda was ahead of him and was opening a drawer opposite the bed.

'Here they are.' She held up his keyring. He felt so helpless, lying there. He should be the one taking care of Magda, not the other way around. But there was a strange comfort in her actions. She was behaving as if they were a married couple.

*

The day passed slowly, marked by visits from the nursing staff checking on him. By early evening, George was feeling much better and was sitting up against a bank of pillows when Magda arrived with his book and a bag of fresh fruit. 'Thought you might like these, too,' she said, holding it up. 'I bumped into Jo and Col downstairs – and Owen and Fran. They weren't sure how many visitors you'd be allowed, so are going to check.'

'Right.' It was lovely to see Magda again, but the thought of the others pouring into the room made him flinch. 'Maybe not all at once,' he said.

As he spoke, Jo and Col appeared. 'We won't stay long, 'Jo said, hovering by the door, 'and Owen and Fran have gone home. The nurse said we shouldn't tire you, but we wanted to make sure you were okay.'

'As well as can be expected. Isn't that what they say?' George managed to chuckle. 'I'm to hear tomorrow when they're going to let me out. Have to see the consultant.'

'Wallace?' Col asked. 'I've heard he's a top man. He'll have you back on your feet in no time.'

'I'm not too sure.' The company was already beginning to tire George. Strange. Magda's company hadn't had that effect and she'd been there almost all morning. He closed his eyes, just for a moment.

'We'll be off, now. Take care and get well. You're in good hands here and I'm sure Magda will take good care of you.' Col ushered Jo out of the room and closed the door behind them.

'It's natural for them to be concerned,' Magda said, taking one of George's hands in hers as if she needed the contact to reassure herself he was alive. 'They were good to me when… when it happened. They brought me here, followed the ambulance, and took me home again. I was in no fit state to drive.'

George thought he saw a bead of moisture in the corner of Magda's eyes. Had she really thought he was a goner? Did she care so much?

'It was kind of them to come. Sorry if I sounded ungrateful.' George sighed. 'I'm not good company. Thanks for bringing my book – and the fruit. Sorry if I don't feel much like talking, but I'm glad to see you. Can you stay for a bit?'

'Of course.'

They sat in silence. From time to time, George dozed off, happy to see Magda still there each time he opened his eyes again. But eventually, she rose to go. 'They're going to kick me out soon, George,' she said, leaning over to kiss him – on the lips this time. How he wished he had the energy to take her in his arms. He wondered idly if anyone had ever made love on one of these hard, narrow, hospital beds. He chuckled to himself. He must be getting better if he was having these thoughts.

Twenty-nine

Magda hated seeing George looking so frail. That's what hospitals did to you. They took away your freedom, made you part of the system; you became a case and ceased to be a person. At least George would be out soon, and she could look after him here, in her home.

Always an early riser, today she'd been up even earlier than usual to check on the horses and give the dogs their morning walk. It had been lovely meandering along the lane as the sun was coming up over the horizon. Today was the summer solstice – an auspicious day for George's return home. Even though Halcyon wasn't his home yet, it would be, as soon as he sold his house in town, something he seemed determined to do, even though Magda suggested he might want to hang on to it as an investment.

Although many traditions had died in ancient times, Magda knew that in other parts of the world, in the Northern hemisphere, the summer solstice – the longest day in the year – was still often celebrated with bonfires, singing, dancing, feasting and rituals, often associated with increasing fertility. Magda chuckled to herself. She and George were well past that phase of their lives, but she was still looking forward to the romance underpinning many of those festivals – to having him back in her bed.

Back home, she left the dogs to roam in the yard while she had breakfast and the cup of peppermint tea with which she liked to start her day. The bedroom was ready with fresh sheets on the bed, the room redolent with the lavender and frankincense fragrances she knew promoted health and wellness. Magda hoped she hadn't overdone it. George didn't understand her affection for essential oils. But at least he didn't rubbish them the way Bill had.

Thinking of her late husband made her stop in her tracks as it always did. What would he think of her and George getting together? As if he was here now, Magda could hear his voice, '*I always knew George was waiting to step into my shoes and my bed. I'm just surprised it took you both so long.*'

At least, Magda reminded herself, the bed was a new one. And no one – not even the gossips in Granite Springs – could accuse them of rushing into anything, not even the ones who'd been so willing to spread rumours about them in the past.

Soon she was driving into town, her heart singing. She was bringing George home. His family were arriving from New Zealand tomorrow. Maybe it would be a good Christmas after all.

*

Magda drove home carefully, very much aware of the precious cargo she was carrying. While appearing better, she knew George still had a long way to go to recover completely. A heart attack wasn't something to treat carelessly, no matter how mild it was deemed to be. All along the way, she threw glances at her passenger from the corner of her eye to ensure he was all right.

'Stop giving me those looks,' George finally said, when they'd been travelling for about half an hour.

'What looks?'

'As if you expect me to die on you. The doc fixed me up. I'm likely to live just as long as you are – maybe longer.'

'Hmm.' But Magda decided to keep her eyes on the road ahead for the remainder of the trip, however difficult she might find it.

As she turned off the main road, she was surprised to see a taxi passing her, turning off the lane back onto the main road. Besides her own house, there were only the Larsens and the Fords who lived along here. She couldn't imagine either of them having to resort to using a taxi. Perhaps the driver had taken a wrong turn.

She thought no more of it as she drove through the gate and up the drive to where the dogs were fussing around something on the veranda. Promising herself to check later, she helped George out of the car, supporting him with one arm despite his protest he could manage on his own.

'Grandma!'

Magda blinked. She couldn't believe her eyes. Standing there beside Caesar and Brutus, wearing a pair of short dungarees and a grubby tee-shirt, her dark hair tied up in a ponytail, was her granddaughter, Holly.

'Holly! What are you doing here? I thought…'

Holly dashed forward to hug Magda and put her arm around George too, helping him into the house. Once there, and with George safely installed in a comfortable armchair, Holly started to speak.

'I was in university when everyone at home got sick. I didn't want to spend Christmas with a houseful of sick people, not even my own family. And we'd planned to come here. I wanted to see you again. I asked Dad to email me my ticket. I also asked him not to tell you. I wanted it to be a surprise. I guess it was more of a surprise than I anticipated.' She gestured to George. 'I'm sorry if I made a mistake.'

'No, my darling. How could your arrival be a mistake? I'm delighted to see you, to think you came all this way by yourself to spend Christmas with your old grandmother. This is George. He's…' What was George? An old friend? Her lover? Her future…? 'He's an old friend, a good friend. He's been in hospital and is spending Christmas here. It's so lovely to see you.' Magda couldn't stifle the thrill at the realisation at least one member of her own family would be spending Christmas with her.

'Let me make us a cup of tea and you can tell me all about it.' Magda went through to the kitchen to boil the electric jug and set out three cups, taking the packet of peppermint tea from the pantry. There was no way she was going to serve George coffee till he was further down the road to recovery. While Magda was making the tea, she heard the hum of conversation and the occasional burst of laughter from the living room where she'd left George and Holly. She smiled at the sound of her two favourite people getting to know each other.

'Now,' she said, when they were all settled with tea and a plate of brownies she'd picked up from The Bean Sprout Café the day before.

'Holly's been telling me how all her family were struck down with food poisoning,' George said. 'You didn't tell me that's why Scott and his family had called off. It wasn't that they didn't want to be here.'

Magda glowed at the news. In the back of her mind there had been the suspicion Scott might have used their sickness as an excuse. How could she have thought that of her son? Quite easily, she realised, given how apart they'd grown over the years. While it was good to know how well he'd done in Canada, the good life he'd made for himself and his family, there was no getting away from the fact that these days, they had little in common.

'And she wants to study drama,' George continued.

Magda stared at Holly. 'I didn't know. Your dad didn't say.'

'Mum and Dad don't approve.' Holly looked down at the floor. 'They don't think there's any future in it. But I know I'd do well. I had the lead in a couple of school plays, and I joined the drama group at uni. But…' her lips turned down, '…I'm dependent on Dad for funding my degree, so I'm stuck with studying business. Business – I ask you!'

'I told her there's a good School of Music and Drama at the William Farrer University right here in Granite Springs,' George said with a wink.

'George! Don't go putting ideas into her head.' But the thought of Holly attending university here in Granite Springs was an attractive one. 'What would Scott have to say about that?'

'He'd probably say you were an interfering old bat,' George chuckled, 'and he wouldn't be far wrong.'

Holly laughed. 'You two. Are you always like this? It's better than the television.'

Magda and George both turned to look at her in dismay. What did she mean?

'Sorry. I don't mean anything bad. I love to listen to you. You sound so… I don't know… so in tune with each other. As if you've been sparring like this for years, as if you forgot I was even here. You're more than just old friends, aren't you?'

Magda sent a pleading look to George.

'This lovely lady has recently agreed to be… not my wife – not yet, anyway – but to be what I believe is called my significant other.'

'Oh, George! What he means, Holly, is that, now he seems to need more care, I've agreed to his ongoing pleading for us to live together. George will be giving up his house in town and moving out here permanently.'

'Oh, Grandma! I'm so pleased. I hated to think of you growing old all by yourself, with only your dogs and horses for company. Dad'll be pleased too. After you left, he said…' She stopped and put a hand over her mouth as if realising she'd said too much.

'It's okay, sweetheart. I always suspected my sons talk about me behind my back. I expect your Uncle Kenny does, too. That's what families do. They mean well. I know they have my best interests at heart. The trouble is, I often have different ideas about what might be in my best interests.' She chuckled. 'Now we need to work out where you're going to sleep. George's family will be arriving from New Zealand tomorrow and I only have two spare rooms.'

'I'm easy. I can kip down anywhere,' Holly said with a grin. 'Your family live in New Zealand?' She turned to George. 'How long have they been there?'

'That's a story for another time,' Magda said, seeing George beginning to tire. 'George should be resting. Let me get him into bed, then we can talk more.'

*

George slept most of the day, allowing Magda to catch up on Holly's news and aspirations. The young girl was eager to know more about the local university and the school George had spoken about and, despite having misgivings, Magda promised to introduce her to Owen and take her to visit the campus after Christmas. Perhaps the girl would have forgotten about it by then, or would be missing her friends and family in Canada.

If Holly did want to make the move, however, Magda knew she'd be willing to help her, even if Scott refused to fund her study in Australia. Then there was the issue of her being eligible to enrol. It was all best put off till later.

It was a coincidence when, on a stroll along the lane with Caesar and Brutus in the late afternoon, they were hailed by Owen who was pushing along the stroller containing his grandson.

As soon as Magda introduced them, Holly exclaimed, 'Owen Larsen. Are you the one who's in charge of drama at the local uni?'

'That's me. Do we have a budding actor here?' he asked Magda.

'Perhaps. Holly's just arrived from Canada to spend Christmas with us. Her parents may not be so keen on the idea.'

'How's George?' Owen leant down to remove Tor's toy dog from Caesar's mouth. 'I heard he was getting home today.'

'He's settling in. He was asleep when we left. He may be up to visitors soon, but best to wait till after Christmas.'

'Will do. Give him our regards. I hear you're going to have a full house for Christmas.'

'I am, more so with Holly here.'

Holly beamed.

'Maybe we can all get together on Boxing Day or later in the week. I know Jo and Col want to put on a big bash.'

Magda remembered Jo had mentioned something about it earlier – when Magda was expecting Kenny and Scott to be here. 'We'll see,' she said.

Back home, Holly wandered off to talk to the horses, saying, 'It's so cool, here, Grandma.'

Magda peeped into the bedroom where George was beginning to stir. She sat on the side of the bed and took his hand in hers. 'You old fraud,' she said. 'You gave me such a fright.' With her free hand, she stroked a strand of hair from his brow. 'I thought I'd lost you.'

'I love you, Magda,' George said, his hand tightening in hers. 'You do know, don't you?'

'I love you, too, George. I want to spend the rest of my days with you. It just took me longer to work it out.'

Thirty

'Are you sure you'll recognise them?' George fretted, as Magda prepared to set off for the airport.

'I've seen their photos. Guy looks just like you,' Magda replied, frustrated at his fussing. He'd been like a cat on a hot tin roof all morning, disappointed he wasn't going to be there to greet Guy and his family personally. 'And they know to expect me. You told them, didn't you?'

'Yeah, but…'

'Don't worry, I won't come home without them. And mind you take care while I'm gone. Don't try to do too much.'

'I'll take care of him, Grandma,' Holly said with a grin. 'I'm going to teach him sudoku.'

'I don't know about that,' George said doubtfully. 'I've always been better with words than numbers. There's nothing wrong with a good crossword.'

'Nothing at all. But you'll love it when you get the hang of it.'

Magda shook her head. But she was delighted how quickly the pair – both so important to her – had taken to each other. Last night, when Holly asked, 'George, Can I call you Grandad?' Magda thought he was going to burst into tears. Instead, he only said, 'Of course you can. Now I'm a grandad twice over.'

*

Granite Springs airport was much busier than usual. It seemed to Magda that half the town were there waiting expectantly for friends and relatives arriving from overseas and interstate for the holiday. For just a moment, she felt a tinge of sadness that she wasn't there to welcome her own family, then she brushed it aside. She had Holly at home, and now that she and George were a couple, he'd assured her his family was hers, too. It wasn't the same, but…

The sound of the large aircraft landing and rolling across the tarmac interrupted her musings. She moved forward with the crowd, eager to catch a glimpse of the man who was the image of the younger George she'd met all those years ago, when she and Bill first got together. Did George have feelings for her even then? Surely not! But the idea he might have harboured an unrequited love for her since Bill died or even before, gave her the strangest feeling inside, as if a love that had been buried deep was now being allowed to unfurl and blossom to the surface. She could only smile at the warmth of it, at how good it made her feel.

Suddenly they were standing in front of her, and she was enveloped in a warm hug from first Guy, then Anita and Oliver. The young man towered over his parents and had to bend down to put his arms round Magda. George would love him.

'How is George?' Guy asked, as they piled into George's car, the boot filled with their luggage. All of them wouldn't have fitted into Magda's little ute, so George had insisted she drive the Prius which she picked up on the way.

'He's pretty good. The trouble is making him take things easy,' Magda replied. 'But I've left him with Holly, my granddaughter. She arrived unexpectedly from Canada yesterday.'

'It's good of you to offer to put us up, but if it's putting you out, we could stay at George's. He has a house in town, doesn't he?' Anita asked.

'He does, but there's room for us all at Halcyon. I've put up a camp bed in my studio. One of the young ones can sleep there.' Remembering the height of Oliver, Magda was glad Holly had offered to take the camp bed. She doubted Oliver would fit on it comfortably.

'Studio? Do you paint?' Anita asked.

'No. It's a massage studio.'

'Massage? How wonderful. Perhaps…'

'I'd be happy to give you one.' Magda chuckled. There were always varied reactions from people when they learnt of what she viewed as her calling.

'You mentioned a granddaughter. How old is she?' Oliver wanted to know.

'Nineteen.'

'Same as me!'

Magda glanced at Oliver in the rearview mirror, wondering how he'd appear to Holly. He was a handsome young man. He was only going to be here for a short time, but things could happen quickly. She hoped he wouldn't break Holly's heart. But then she checked herself, realising that she was the one all loved-up. It might be the season of love and goodwill to all men, but she had no right to go assuming romance in others.

The trip back to Halcyon seemed longer than usual with both Guy and Anita commenting on the scenery on the way and comparing the dry paddocks to the lush ones they'd left in New Zealand. Oliver remained silent, lost in his thoughts.

As she pulled in, Magda could see George and Holly sitting on the veranda, the dogs at their feet. As soon as they saw the car, the dogs jumped up and ran towards it, almost knocking Magda over when she got out.

'Wow!' Oliver stepped out of the car, put his hands on his hips and gazed around. 'I hadn't realised you lived in such a beautiful spot. This is magic. Where's…?'

He turned to his father, but Guy had already hurried over to where George was walking slowly towards them with tears in his eyes. Their reunion brought a tear to Magda's eyes, too. How could she have felt resentful of George's family? How could she have wanted to deny him this pleasure?

Guy drew Anita over to meet George and the pair hugged.

Suddenly Magda became aware of Holly and Oliver staring at each other.

'You must be Oliver,' Holly said.

'And you're the granddaughter from Canada.'

They smiled at each other, and Magda was transported back in time to when she and Bill met. She had the strangest feeling… no, it was more than just a feeling, it was a *knowing*. An overwhelming knowing that she was seeing the beginning of something that would have wide-ranging repercussions and would bind the two families together more than ever.

Thirty-one

Next day was Christmas Eve and everyone gathered in the kitchen for breakfast. Magda provided a variety of cereals and fruit along with yoghurt, hoping no one wanted a cooked breakfast. She had a lot to do today in preparation for Christmas Day and wanted to give George time to get to know Guy and his family.

'I have to go into town to rescue the food George bought for Christmas,' she said, when everyone had finished eating and Guy and Anita were on their second cups of coffee. The two younger members of the group had finished earlier, and Holly had taken Oliver out to see the horses, promising Magda she'd check on the water trough while they were there. 'I'm sure you and George have a lot to catch up on.'

'Can I help?' Anita asked. 'The men don't need me here, and I'd like to see around the town. It looked choice when we drove through yesterday.'

'Oh!' It hadn't occurred to Magda, but she could probably do with some help, and perhaps Anita wanted to leave Guy and George on their own for a bit. 'That would be good,' she said. 'We might stop off for a cup of tea or coffee while we're there. The Bean Sprout is a favourite café of mine and I want to pick up a box of Marie's brownies. 'You men will be fine on your own?' She gave George a wink.

'Can you pick up those other things I mentioned, Magda?' George asked, an anxious expression on his face.

'No worries.' Before they rose this morning, George had given her clear instructions where to find the gifts he'd wrapped, along with the photo book he was so proud of. She hoped Guy appreciated how much this visit meant to him. But, seeing the way the younger man's eyes lit up when he looked at his father, she knew it meant a lot to him, too.

The drive to town was enjoyable. Anita proved to be more talkative without her husband and son, and by the time they reached Granite Springs, Magda had learned their family history. Oliver was in his first year at university studying viticulture, having refused to follow his dad into medicine. It was his dream to own his own vineyard one day. Anita herself was a high school drama teacher.

'You must speak with Holly,' Magda said, once they'd reached town and were seated in The Bean Sprout Café, Magda with a pot of lemon and ginger tea, and Anita with a cappuccino. 'She wants to study drama, but her father is against it. Now she's discovered we have a School of Music and Drama right here in Granite Springs, I think she has ideas of moving here.'

'The town has a university?'

'A good one, I'm told. One of my neighbours is a professor there – in the School of Music and Drama as it happens.' She laughed, and Anita joined in.

'Today's young people,' Anita said. 'They have their own ideas of what they intend to do with their lives. They don't want to listen to us. Since we discovered George, Oliver has been talking about transferring to an Australian university. I don't suppose they have a School of Viticulture at your Granite Springs University?' she chuckled.

'You know, I believe they do! Its proper title is Willian Farrer University. You can look it up.'

'I expect Ollie has done that already. He's really taken with the idea of having a new grandfather. It was hard for him when first my dad, then Guy's, passed away. Guy's finding out about George when his mum died was a shock – but a good one'

Magda liked Anita. Although she'd been reluctant to accept the idea of George having a family of his own, now she'd met them, she had to admit they were lovely people.

'I'm glad George has you,' Anita said, surprising Magda out of her reverie. 'When Guy heard he'd never married, he was worried he'd never got over Rose. She was a lovely lady, a good wife and mother, but…'

'You knew her well?' Magda was curious.

'Pretty well. She could be easy to get along with but did have some definite opinions. Guy and his dad had to toe the line.'

Magda's ears pricked up. Was she about to hear gossip about the woman who'd abandoned George, stolen his future and his son?

'She had her failings. I guess we all do. But Rose had a way of manipulating people to make them do what she wanted. Sometimes it was for their own benefit, but sometimes… it wasn't nice.' She sighed. 'I'm afraid I wasn't one of her favourite people and I didn't always follow her rules for how Oliver should be brought up.'

'He seems a nice boy.'

'Thanks. He is. But if his grandmother had had her way… Sorry, you don't want to hear all this old family stuff.'

Not usually one to gossip, Magda was fascinated by this insight into George's old flame. Perhaps he'd had a lucky escape after all.

'It was sad when she became so ill, then…' She sighed again. 'But we're here now, and there's no sense in dwelling on the past. George is a lovely man.'

'He is.'

'About George. He and Guy had a bit of a chat yesterday – about the trip he was to make with us.'

'Oh, yes.' Magda had been trying to forget about the trip. Surely George wouldn't want to go now.

'He decided, rightly I think, that New Year in Sydney would be too much for him. It's a pity as he was looking forward to it. But the Noosa part of the trip – he thinks he could manage to join us there. It'll be a relaxing week.'

Magda felt her heart sink, her earlier reservations reasserting themselves again.

'So Guy and I were thinking…' Anita tipped her head to one side and gave Magda a cautious glance, '…how would you like to come too – and Holly, of course, if she's still here.'

Magda didn't know what to say. Here she was, harbouring feelings of jealousy, when all the time George's family were making an effort to include her.

'But surely it's too late to change the bookings,' was all she could think of, her heart beating madly at the thought of spending a week in a tropical paradise in Queensland with George and these lovely people.

'Not at all. We've rented a house, so there will be plenty of room, and I'm sure we can arrange flights. You will come, won't you?'

'Yes. Thanks so much. And I'm sure Holly will be delighted too, though I don't know her plans.' What more could she say?

*

'This is George's house.' Magda pulled the car into the driveway of the familiar old redbrick home. 'He's lived here all of his life. It belonged to his parents, and he came back to it after university, after…'

'After Rose came back home,' Anita said sadly. 'I guess we'll never know why she did what she did, but I'm sure she had her reasons.'

They were inside the house by now, and Magda headed straight for the kitchen where many of George's purchases were still sitting in their supermarket bags. 'There should be an esky,' she muttered, finding it sitting next to the back door. 'I'll pack the perishables from the fridge into it, if you can carry those bags out to the ute.'

While Anita was gone, Magda made a trip into the bedroom where George had hidden his Christmas gifts in the wardrobe. Fortunately, they were all already wrapped. She found a box and loaded them into it.

'It's a lovely house,' Anita said when she returned. 'Reminds me of something I saw on television. I can't remember the name of the programme. It's very different from the bungalow we have back home. Your house is different, too. Will you be moving into town? Sorry,' she said, seeing Magda's look of astonishment. 'I know it's none of my business, but I just assumed…'

Magda laid down the box she was carrying and put a hand on the back of a chair. 'You're right in thinking we plan to move in together, but George will be moving out to Halcyon. There are my animals to consider.'

'Of course. It just seems such a pity…' She gazed around the old-fashioned family kitchen.

For the first time, Magda realised what she was asking George to give up – what he was willing to give up for her. This was his family's home. It had been in the Turnbull family for generations. Was that less important than her acreage and her animals? She rubbed a hand across her forehead. What was she thinking? She and George had discussed this. They'd agreed.

'There are a lot of houses like this in Granite Springs,' she said, hoping she didn't sound dismissive.

But as they drove back home, Magda mentally chastised herself. She'd been worried Guy didn't appreciate how much he meant to George, while being oblivious of how much *she* meant to him.

Thirty-two

Christmas day promised to be another hot one, making Magda glad she'd planned a cold lunch and had done most of the cooking the day before. Everything was ready for the day, the house filled with the scent of pine and the fragrant candles she had placed on several shelves and surfaces.

Breakfast today was a leisurely affair. Holly and Oliver had taken over the kitchen and produced platters of mangoes, pancakes and waffles, which they then carried into the living room. Everyone gathered around the tree under which piles of parcels had magically appeared overnight.

The present-opening was a riotous affair, and Magda and George watched with amusement as Holly and Oliver bickered as if they'd known each other for years. To George's delight, Guy and Oliver went into raptures over the photo book, insisting he give them a full account on when and where each of the photos had been taken.

'What's the plan for today?' Guy asked, when everyone but Magda was drinking coffee and she was enjoying her usual cup of peppermint tea.

'If George is up to it, I thought we might take a wander along the lane,' Magda said. 'It'll give you an idea of the countryside around here, and I normally take the dogs for a walk around now. Then we can have lunch. I haven't planned anything else.'

'Is there anything I can do to help with lunch?' Anita asked.

'You did all that was needed yesterday.'

After they'd returned from town, Magda and Anita had banished everyone from the kitchen while they cooked the ham and turkey and prepared the salads for today's lunch. All that was needed now was to take everything out of the fridge and set up the table on the veranda.

'Let's do it, then,' Guy said. 'Are you up for it, George?'

'I think I can manage a short walk. Magda can bring me back when I run out of energy.'

Magda gave him a worried look. Was he trying to do too much? But his cheerful grin belied his words.

As they walked along, the dogs running back and forth between them, the group split into couples. George walked with Guy, Magda with Anita, and Holly with Oliver. Magda noticed Holly slip her hand into Oliver's as the two rushed ahead, commenting loudly at the sight of first, Owen's goats, then, Col's alpacas.

'I think I've had enough.' George turned back towards Magda. 'If you keep going, you can walk right around the block,' he said to the others.

Relieved George had decided to turn back, Magda took his arm and, leaving the younger members of the party to continue, they headed for home. Caesar and Brutus, confused by the division of the group, ran one way, then another, before deciding to join Magda and George and return to Halcyon.

'They're lovely,' Magda said. 'Your family. I'm so glad for you, George.' She squeezed his arm. 'I'm sorry I didn't share your excitement when you discovered Guy. It was wrong of me. I was selfish. I wanted you all to myself. I see now it was jealousy, not something I'm proud of.'

'That's okay, my dear.' George's eyes crinkled in amusement. 'Shows me you really cared for me – more than you might have imagined.'

'You could be right,' she chuckled, as they reached the gate. 'Now, why don't you have a lie down before lunch?'

'Only if you join me.' George winked and gave a chuckle. 'I'm really liking that big bed of yours.'

'I don't think…' Magda began, but why not? It would take the others at least an hour to make the circuit of the block, and lunch was all prepared.

And… it was Christmas.

They giggled like a pair of teenagers as they reached the house and headed for the bedroom.

*

Lunch over, everyone was relaxing when Holly said, 'I have a surprise. Won't be long.' She disappeared inside, Oliver at her heels, leaving the others bemused.

Only a few minutes later, the two reappeared.

'You need to come into the living room now.' Holly had a big grin on her face.

Once there, Holly and Oliver arranged everyone in seats around the large-screen television, an extravagant gift from Kenny Magda rarely watched.

She noticed Holly had connected her laptop to the television and was doing something with the keyboard. Holly clicked on the control and the laptop screensaver appeared on the television screen. Then the screen changed.

'It's Zoom,' Guy said. 'We use the software at work sometimes for consultations with specialists.

'But what…?' Magda began.

'Wait and see.' Holly was suffused with excitement. She pressed a few keys, then…

'It's your dad… and Kenny,' Magda said in surprise as first Scott's, then Kenny's face appeared on the screen.

'Merry Christmas,' they both said at once.

'Merry Christmas,' Magda replied, almost too overcome to speak. 'How did Holly set this up?'

'I contacted Dad and Uncle Kenny yesterday. They thought it was a good idea. So I managed to set up the meeting. We only have forty minutes, so you'll have to be quick if everyone wants to speak.'

The forty minutes passed in a flash. Seeing both her sons and her grandchildren brought tears to Magda's eyes. She was able to introduce George's family to hers, something she'd never imagined being able to do. It was almost as if they were all in the room together. Although at times everyone tried to speak at once, they gradually worked it out and were able to enjoy the conversation.

'What a wonderful idea, Holly,' Magda said, when the faces on the screen disappeared.

'It was actually Oliver who thought of it,' Holly admitted. 'When I told him how I'd miss being with Mum and Dad and Chloe today. It was a good idea, wasn't it?'

'The best. Thanks, Oliver.' Magda turned to the young man who was looking embarrassed.

'It was so lovely to meet your family, Magda,' Anita said. 'I feel we've been accepted by you and them. I know Guy and Oliver must, too.'

Guy nodded, and Magda looked over to where Holly and Oliver were sitting with their heads together.

'I think it may be time for celebration. Oliver!' Guy said, rising and going to the kitchen with his son.

A few moments later, they returned, Guy carrying two bottles of champagne, and Oliver a tray containing six glasses. He opened the bottle with a loud pop and filled the glasses.

'To finding George,' he said. 'To George and Magda. And to our new family.' He raised his own glass towards George and Magda.

George bent over to whisper in Magda's ear.

Her eyes twinkled with delight.

'Yes,' she said without hesitation, 'Yes, I will

THE END

If you've enjoyed Magda's story, I'd really appreciate it if you could leave a review. A few words will suffice, no need for a lengthy review. It will mean a lot to me and help other readers find my books.

Look out for the next in the Granite Springs series,
The Life She Creates.

Can Granite Springs provide healing and a new beginning?

Peta Forrest has arrived in the country town of Granite Springs determined to help her granddaughter cope with her mother's brutal murder and create a new life for them both.

Frank Beattie, owner of The Bean Sprout Café, has finally accepted that his ex has moved on, and so should he. He finds himself drawn to the town's new arrival – a woman whose vulnerability calls out to him.

While Frank piques Peta's interest, her courage and energy are channelled into a dilemma she hadn't anticipated – fighting for the right to care for her granddaughter.

Tempted to lean on Frank for support, she's not convinced he's over his ex and is wary of becoming involved.

Can Peta create the new life she's seeking, and will Frank find the happiness he deserves?

You can order it here: getbook.at/TheLifeSheCreates

Dear Reader,

First, I'd like to thank you for choosing to read *A Granite Springs Christmas* Magda has featured as a minor character in several of the earlier books, so I decided she needed her own story and her own happy ending. And what better than to make her book my first Christmas story?

Having spent seven years teaching university and living in an Australian country town, and don an acreage, I've enjoyed writing a series with a rural setting and drawing on my experience of living in the country – with goats – and teaching in university. This is the fifth book in the series set in the fictional country town of Granite Springs and I'm thrilled by the response of you, my readers, to this series, how you tell me my characters are real people you'd love to have as friends. I feel they're my friends too, and they've become a part of my life. I hope you've enjoyed meeting Magda and George.

If you'd like to stay up to date with my new releases and special offers you can sign up to my reader's group.

You can sign up here
https://mailchi.mp/f5cbde96a5e6/maggiechristensensreadersgroup

I'll never share your email address, and you can unsubscribe at any time. You can also contact me via Facebook Twitter or by email. I love hearing from my readers and will always reply.

Thanks again.

Acknowledgements

As always, this book could not have been written without the help and advice of a number of people.

Firstly, my husband Jim for listening to my plotlines without complaint, for his patience and insights as I discuss my characters and storyline with him, for his patience and help with difficult passages and advice on my male dialogue, and for being there when I need him.

John Hudspith, editor extraordinaire for his ideas, suggestions, encouragement and attention to detail.

Jane Dixon-Smith for her patience and for working her magic on my beautiful cover and interior.

My thanks also to early readers of this book —Helen, Maggie and Louise, for their helpful comments and advice. Also to Annie of *Annie's books at Peregian* and Graeme of *The Bookshop at Caloundra* for their ongoing support,

And to all of my readers. Your support and comments make it all worthwhile. I'm thrilled you enjoy my more mature characters and that the situations they find themselves in resonate with you.

About the Author

After a career in education, Maggie Christensen began writing contemporary women's fiction portraying mature women facing life-changing situations. Her travels inspire her writing, be it her trips to visit family in Scotland, in Oregon, USA or her home on Queensland's beautiful Sunshine Coast. Maggie writes of mature heroines coming to terms with changes in their lives and the heroes worthy of them. Her writing has been described by one reviewer as *like a nice warm cup of tea. It is warm, nourishing, comforting and embracing.*

From her native Glasgow, Scotland, Maggie was lured by the call 'Come and teach in the sun' to Australia, where she worked as a primary school teacher, university lecturer and in educational management. Now living with her husband of over thirty years on Queensland's Sunshine Coast, she loves walking on the deserted beach in the early mornings and having coffee by the river on weekends. Her days are spent surrounded by books, either reading or writing them – her idea of heaven!

She continues her love of books as a volunteer with her local library where she selects and delivers books to the housebound.

Maggie can be found on Facebook, Twitter, Goodreads, Instagram or on her website.

www.facebook.com/maggiechristensenauthor
www.twitter.com/MaggieChriste33
www.goodreads.com/author/show/8120020.Maggie_Christensen
www.instagram.com/maggiechriste33/
maggiechristensenauthor.com/